D1626561

BOOK LINK

MAL
RTGI

ROTHERHAM LIBRARY & INFORMATION SERVICE

Tel: 01709 815123

1 8 APR 2013

LORD	BOWDEN	Taylor
1 6 MAY 2013	2 7 MAR 2014	- 5 FEB 2015
KNAPTON	Warlington	Outram
JUN 2013	MAY 2014	NAYLOR
RADCLIFFE		0 6 MAR 2019
CHAPMAN	1 5 JUL 2014	ROE
EVANS	DOUGLAS	17/5/19
2 1 NOV 2013	2 8 JUN 2014	
MILLERY	OUTRAM	Accroy
2 3 JAN 2014	Myers	2LD
WHALEY	NOV 2014	
2 1 FEB 2014	SCARKBRICK	
	2 2 DEC 2014	

This book must be returned by the date specified at the time of issue as
the DATE DUE FOR RETURN.
The loan may be extended (personally, by post, telephone or online) for
a further period if the book is not required by another reader, by quoting
the above number / author / title.

Enquiries: 01709 336774

www.rotherham.gov.uk/libraries

Just this once, please be sensible and safe. I've already lost one man in our lives because he was a hero. I can't lose another.

She wanted to stop him, to hold on to him and hug him, to tell him not to do anything stupid, but he wasn't going to listen. Knowing that didn't prevent the words that spilled out of her mouth.

'So you'll rush out into the water, regardless of your own safety? Never mind anyone else. Never mind the people who care about you. Like a damned hero.'

Ben stepped close and leaned near, so that only she heard the anger in his voice. 'It's not your place to be talking to me like this, Doc.'

Dear Reader

The Cook Islands are magical, and to spend a few days relaxing in Rarotonga is what dreams are made of. The first time I visited was with my husband, to attend a wedding. Nearly forty of us made the journey across from New Zealand, and we had so much fun that we went back a year later with our family. The beaches, the warmth, the motor scooters that we all learned to ride (and which I drove into the garden by mistake, because there's no difference between the throttle and the brake) all added up to a package of fun.

This tiny nation is the perfect backdrop for Rachel and Ben's story. Two bruised souls looking to move forward but afraid to take big steps. And what gets bigger than falling in love? Where better for them to test the waters of that love than here, where not a lot happens and everyone is very laid-back?

For Rachel the contrast with working in a hospital in the winter of London couldn't be bigger. For Ben the Cook Islands are also very different from his native New Zealand. The slower pace and fewer big-time criminals make policing very different from back home. It also gives him the opportunity to ponder whether he could revert back to the medical career he abandoned two years earlier.

I hope you enjoy this story.

Cheers!

Sue MacKay

www.suemackay.co.nz

EVERY BOY'S DREAM DAD

BY
SUE MacKAY

All the characters in this book have no existence outside the imagination of the author, and have no relation whatsoever to anyone bearing the same name or names. They are not even distantly inspired by any individual known or unknown to the author, and all the incidents are pure invention.

All Rights Reserved including the right of reproduction in whole or in part in any form. This edition is published by arrangement with Harlequin Enterprises II BV/S.à.r.l. The text of this publication or any part thereof may not be reproduced or transmitted in any form or by any means, electronic or mechanical, including photocopying, recording, storage in an information retrieval system, or otherwise, without the written permission of the publisher.

® and TM are trademarks owned and used by the trademark owner and/or its licensee. Trademarks marked with ® are registered with the United Kingdom Patent Office and/or the Office for Harmonisation in the Internal Market and in other countries.

First published in Great Britain 2012
by Mills & Boon, an imprint of Harlequin (UK) Limited.
Large Print edition 2013
Harlequin (UK) Limited, Eton House,
18-24 Paradise Road, Richmond, Surrey TW9 1SR

© Sue MacKay 2012

ISBN: 978 0 263 23089 5

Harlequin (UK) policy is to use papers that are natural, renewable and recyclable products and made from wood grown in sustainable forests. The logging and manufacturing process conform to the legal environmental regulations of the country of origin.

Printed and bound in Great Britain
by CPI Antony Rowe, Chippenham, Wiltshire

With a background of working in medical laboratories and a love of the romance genre, it is no surprise that **Sue MacKay** writes Medical Romance stories. An avid reader all her life, she wrote her first story at age eight—about a prince, of course. She lives with her own hero in the beautiful Marlborough Sounds, at the top of New Zealand's South Island, where she indulges her passions for the outdoors, the sea and cycling.

Also by Sue MacKay:

THE DANGERS OF DATING YOUR BOSS
SURGEON IN A WEDDING DRESS
RETURN OF THE MAVERICK
PLAYBOY DOCTOR TO DOTING DAD
THEIR MARRIAGE MIRACLE

**These books are also available in eBook format
from www.millsandboon.co.uk**

ROTHERHAM LIBRARY &
INFORMATION SERVICES

B52008087

R00054679

Once again to Lindsay, a big thank you
for your endless support and encouragement.
You are my very own romantic story.

CHAPTER ONE

KNOCK. Knock. Bang. Bang.

Rachel grimaced as the pounding on her front door grew heavier with each passing second. It matched the thumping behind her eyes. 'Not now. Please. I'm all peopled out for the day.' There'd been a continuous stream of welcoming locals since sunrise—which came incredibly early in the Cook Islands. She sighed.

Thud. Thud. Thud.

She huffed out an exasperated breath. Whoever was out there hadn't received her telepathic message. She'd have to tell them straight to their face to go away.

Rachel didn't bother with a smile as she swung the door wide. 'Yes?'

The harsh glare of the overhead light made her blink. But she couldn't blame the light for her throat abruptly closing up, or for how the heat-induced moisture on her skin that had plagued her all day suddenly dried.

On her front step stood a human behemoth. So what? She was used to big men. They held no thrall for her. So why the sudden lurch in her tummy? The quickening of her blood? *Forget it, Rachel.* She had no desire to hook up with anyone any time soon, if ever. Her new start in life did not include finding a soulmate. Or even a playmate. It was meant to be about finding peace and forgiveness, about letting go the despair that had kept her in a holding pattern for nearly two years.

But this man did have a body to drool over. He'd need to turn sideways to fit through her door. Not that he would be gaining access tonight. Or any other day or night. She tried swallowing, but she couldn't.

'She's cut herself.' A deep rumble shook her. 'And got a black eye.'

'What?' Finally she noticed the tiny island lady in the man's arms. Blood coursed down the wounded woman's thigh to drip on to Rachel's step.

'You're Dr Simmonds,' her male visitor rumbled again.

No, right now she was a weary mother with a bewildered little boy whom she'd only just managed to settle for the night. Tomorrow she'd be the doctor everyone was waiting for. 'You need to take her to the hospital.'

'You're closer.'

How did he know who she was? She'd arrived in Rarotonga only two days ago. Of course. The community grapevine, and the many locals who'd paid her their respects throughout the day. Her sluggish, aching brain wasn't operating very well right now. Not when her bed beckoned so invitingly at the ridiculously early hour of eight o'clock. It had been a long and busy day that had started a little after four in the morning when roosters in the vicinity of the house had begun crowing.

Her visitor stood waiting, his gaze demanding her attention as he held the wounded woman.

Black eyes, sharp and intense. Eyes that wouldn't miss a thing, including that she wanted him gone.

Resigned to the fact he wasn't taking the hint to disappear, Rachel stepped back. She couldn't withhold her help—being a doctor wasn't something she switched on and off as it suited her. She never refused aid to anybody needing her medical skills. Anyway, it was her new role in this small nation to look after the woman. 'Take her through to the lounge.'

'Yes, Doc.' The man carried his load with ease, and placed the silent woman on the couch with heart-wrenching gentleness.

There went the clean cover. So much for washing it earlier. She'd be doing it again in the morning. Rachel flicked on the light and shook her head. So much for remembering to buy light bulbs with decent wattage while at the supermarket earlier. Not that she'd been going to spend time in this room tonight so the gloom hadn't been a problem—until now. Kneeling beside the couch, she spoke softly to her patient. 'I'm Rachel Simmonds, the new doctor.'

The woman opened one eye—the other was swollen closed—and studied Rachel curiously for a few moments before the eyelid drooped shut. But not before Rachel noted the pain lurking in that enormous brown orb. One cheek bled slightly from deep scratches. Twisting her head around, she asked the man, 'Do you know what happened?'

'She's dazed. Might've been unconscious briefly.'

His accent sounded similar to what she'd heard locally these past couple of days but he didn't look like an islander. His skin was suntanned rather than naturally brown. His big frame was all lean, well-honed muscle. She asked, 'Where are you from?'

An exasperated sigh, followed by a begrudging answer. 'Next door.'

Right, so he didn't do friendly. Odd for around here, but who was she to complain? Her own temperament didn't go all-out friendly these days. Then she really heard what he'd said. He was her neighbour. Gulp. So they'd probably see a bit of each other. Rare excitement fizzed across her skin. *Reality check, Rach.* Why would she be seeing much of this guy? He had a life, probably one that included a wife and kids. But she'd been told that in the Cook Islands there was no such thing as aloofness, no such thing as a stranger. So there'd be waves and hellos over the fence as they all went about their daily lives. Nothing like her old life in London, then.

With a flick of her head she returned her attention to the woman. Hopefully she'd be able to patch her up and send them both on their way quickly. But there were things Rachel needed to know. 'What do you think caused the wound? Did you see it happen?' she asked.

'Found her lying on the kitchen floor when I got home. It looked like she slipped. She'd been mopping.'

Wow. Getting more vocal. Just. Rachel bit down a retort and straightened up, locking eyes with him. 'So she's not your partner?'

He shook his head. 'My housekeeper.'

No wife, then? Or one who worked long hours and didn't do housework? Rachel pulled back as hope flared that he might be single. Wrong, wrong, wrong. 'I'll need my medical kit.' As she turned around, the police insignia on the sleeve of his blue shirt registered in her brain. Blimey, was she awake enough to deal with a patient if she'd missed that? 'You're a cop.'

He raised his eyebrows as though to say *Yeah, what took you so long?*—but said nothing.

'Daddy?'

Rachel spun around to face the door, her heart thumping at the sound of hope in her son's voice. 'Riley, sweetheart.' Every time Riley made this mistake she had to let him down, hurt him all over again. When would it stop? When would he finally come to understand that he'd never see his daddy again? The endless expectation that his father would walk through the door one night had driven her to shift halfway around the world in an attempt to get him past that hurdle. 'Riley, you're meant to be in bed, fast asleep.'

'Daddy.' Her son stood hesitantly in the doorway, his head tipped back as he stared up expectantly at the man dominating the lounge. He waited for some recognition, desperate to be lifted up and hugged by those strong arms. Riley could be forgiven his mistake. In the dull light she understood how a small boy might think the cop was his father, given both men were tall and broad, both had short, straight black hair and both wore police uniforms. At least this guy did. And Riley's dad used to.

'No, love. Not Daddy.' She swept Riley up into her arms. The uncertainty in his eyes, the longing, the bewilderment broke Rachel's heart all over. And cranked up the ever-present resentment at her late husband for dying. If Jamie stepped into the room right now she'd kill him all over again.

Riley shrunk into her chest, slid his arms around her neck. 'I'm tired, Mummy.'

'Let's put you back to bed.' They'd have to repeat the ritual of reading his favourite story before he'd agree to go to sleep in this new house, this new country, so far from home and everything familiar.

She glanced across at the woman lying waiting, her good eye still screwed tightly shut. The blood loss from the thigh wounds had slowed to an ooze. Nothing urgent but this poor woman still required her understanding and care.

Rachel pressed Riley's head harder into her breast so he wouldn't see the unpleasant sight he'd so far not noticed. He was distressed enough without having to face up to a woman lying in bloody, torn clothes on the couch. She turned to leave the room.

'I can put him to bed.' The deep voice caught at her, jinking her attention sideways.

'He doesn't go to strangers.' Not since the day his father had died. Jamie's police colleagues had swamped Riley with the best of intentions of being kind and friendly to a hero's son. But unfortunately Riley now associated friendly strangers with the disappearance of his father.

'Riley.' The deep, rumbling voice became softer, gentler, coaxing. 'Want me to read you a story?'

Against her chest Riley's head lifted, nodded once. Dumbfounded, Rachel stared at her son, then across at this man who'd managed to get such a positive response. Without any effort. 'Who are you?' she whispered.

'Ben Armstrong, Senior Constable, Cook Islands Police Department.'

Now she got the accent. Kiwi. Like her best friend, Lissie, who'd wangled an obstetrics job for her at the local hospital where there never used to be an obstetrician. Lissie, who'd also arranged this house for her to rent, having believed it was time Rachel moved on and made a new life for herself and Riley away from that big, empty apartment back in London.

Ben Armstrong held his hands out to Riley, who slowly shifted his weight and stretched to meet his new friend.

Amazed, Rachel handed her son over and muttered around a lump in her throat, 'Second room on the right.' She watched Ben's large hands as he gently held her boy. Envy uncurled in her comfort-starved body. She'd love to be the one being held against that broad expanse of chest.

'Have you got a book?' he asked.

Somehow she managed to hear the question above the thudding in her ears and even gave a sensible answer. 'On the bedside table.'

As the cop strode out of the room, Riley still didn't say a word or make any sound. This wouldn't work. Any moment now her son would realise what was happening and call out for her. All the more reason to hurry. Hefting her medical bag from the corner of the room, she went towards her patient.

Hot. Hot. Hot. Ben suppressed the urge to run his finger under his open collar. Dr Rachel Simmonds was something to be reckoned with.

Or would be if he was remotely interested in getting to know her. Which he absolutely was not. But, phew, she could set an iceberg on fire. What chance did his dormant hormones have of remaining indifferent? She stood tall and slim. Too slim. Except for the deep shadows staining her skin her face was very pale, delicate. Until she opened her mouth. Then she was very res-olute. An intriguing, exciting combination that had already tripped a few switches within his brain. So his brain was below his belt these days? Why wouldn't it be? When those eyes that reminded him of the wild bluebells growing on the family farm back home had rested on him he'd felt as though he'd been raked with a fire iron. Scorched. Seared. Sizzled.

She was a looker. That exquisite, fine-featured face, those big eyes laden with sadness, and the wildly curly hair that wasn't quite blonde or brown haphazardly tied up with a gold ribbon: they all added up to a very neat and enticing package. Then there was the English accent that made him melt inside. She'd turn heads wherever she went, no doubt about it.

But his head would stay firmly facing in the right direction. Away from the new doc. He'd managed to avoid any sort of entanglement since… Pain sliced through his heart. Since that awful night that had turned his world upside down for ever. He leant into the agony. Anguish was good. It focused him, underlined his resolve should it look like faltering. Which it wasn't going to do. Certainly not after just a few minutes in the company of one beautiful, sexy and very single-minded lady. One who was here for a year at the most.

'Will you read my favourite story?' The kid in his arms wriggled to be set down.

Ben shook his head clear of thoughts of the boy's mother and placed Riley on his bed. 'Sure. Which one?'

'That one.' Riley pointed to the top of a pile of well-thumbed books. 'It's about a naughty goat that eats the clothes off the washing line.' The kid clambered over the bed, getting comfortable.

Ben noted all the pictures on the walls, the soccer ball in the corner, the stuffed toys on top of the set of drawers. He could have had a child with a room like this if he and Catrina had been given more time. If she hadn't driven that night. If he'd been able to save her.

Don't go there. Ben squeezed his eyes tight, trying to blank out Catrina's last staccato breaths. The sight of her beloved face suddenly contorted with pain and illuminated by flickering red and blue from the emergency services' lights. He tried to empty out the fear and helplessness that had paralysed him that night and which returned to grip him, squeeze him, whenever he thought about her.

He counted to ten.

Finally, finally, he managed to refocus on the boy's room, and asked in a voice he didn't recognise, 'How old are you?'

'Nearly five.' The kid was concentrating on his book, turning the pages as he said, 'I want to start school soon with my friend Harry. His brother, Jason, already goes.'

'It's good to have friends in a new place.'

'Their mother is Lissie. She's Mummy's friend.'

'I heard.' Lissie was a newly appointed general surgeon from Auckland via London who had come to Rarotonga with her Cook Islands husband and their two boys. The community was lucky to have her. Her husband had come home to run his family's boat-charter business since his father had had a stroke.

Already Lissie had been instrumental in getting a position created at the local hospital for women's health after the death of her sister-in-law from cervical cancer. The woman had not wanted to see a local male doctor when symptoms had first presented, and by the time she'd given in and had an exam it had been too late.

The new obstetrician, this kid's mum, would be heading up the much-needed new department as a trial for the next year.

'Don't you want to read to me now?' Tears blurred Riley's voice.

Ben perched on the edge of the bed and took the book from Riley's willing hands. 'Sorry, little fella. Of course I do.'

This boy obviously needed a father figure. Where was his old man? Had the doc done a runner? He'd nearly freaked out when Riley had called him Daddy—it made him want to escape the doc's house, and getting Effie patched up would speed his departure. So here he was, about to read a story to her kid. Talk about getting very close very quickly to a little family he didn't want anything to do with. Something deep inside told him the doc and her kid had the potential to draw him into their lives—which went directly against everything he believed in now. He ran solo in this world. It was the only way to get by.

'I can read the story.' The kid's high-pitched voice cracked into Ben's brain as the book was tugged from his grasp.

Okay, the kid didn't need him here. Ben began to rise.

'"Willy, the goat, likes to eat."' The kid's voice wobbled.

Ben paused, half off the bed.

The boy turned the page. '"Willy eats everything."'

Ben sank back down.

Another page was turned. '"Willy eats the flowers in the garden."' The kid peeped up at Ben. 'Do you like this story?'

Ben's heart rolled under his ribs at the insecurity in the kid's eyes. No child deserved to feel like that. 'Yes.'

Riley's face split with a huge yawn. Ben took the book, began reading from the next page, and within minutes the kid was asleep. Ben tucked the sheet up to his little chin and stood looking down at him, wondering what sort of life he'd come from, and what the future held for him.

Enough. Get out of here. Start thinking like that and next thing he'd know he'd be involved in the kid's life. And the doc's.

Stalking down the short hall he marvelled at all the boxes still to be unpacked. There were plenty more in the lounge too. Had the doc cleared out Harrod's before she'd left England? The only room that appeared set up and completely free of clutter was the kid's. Obviously the doc put making her son feel comfortable in his new surroundings first. Ben nodded to himself. So she was a good mother. Let's see if she was a good doctor.

If only Effie hadn't needed stitches he'd have dealt with her injuries and saved coming over here at all. But from the moment he'd found Effie it had been apparent she needed qualified medical care. He should've put her in the car and driven to the hospital. It wasn't exactly far. But he'd had a brainless moment and decided Effie should see the new doctor as soon as possible. The women might as well get to know each other; they might be seeing a bit of one another over the fence in the months to come. He'd done right by his housekeeper bringing her here.

But face it, he was intrigued. What was the doc's history? She'd travelled a big distance for a job in a second-rate hospital when, as a specialist, she could surely command a good position at any modern hospital with all the bells and whistles. Not to mention the huge salary that would go with such a placement. The Cook Islands didn't usually attract highly qualified people willing to work for very little remuneration. Mostly the foreigners were Kiwis who came on holiday, thought they'd found a slice of heaven and stayed on for a year or two. But eventually most of them left again. As would the doc. He'd bet his rust bucket of a car on that. At least she wouldn't find the local hospital lacking in good spirits and meaningful intentions. There was a brilliant crew up there.

Did the deep sadness darkening the doc's eyes have anything to do with choosing such a remote part of the world to move to? Probably. That sadness made him yearn to reach out to her, pull her close in a hug. He wanted to banish that sorrow and bring laughter and light to her face. *Hell, man, she didn't come all this way to have you interfere in her life. You spend your time avoiding other people's pain—why do you want to know about the doc's problems?*

Suddenly light-headed, he leaned against the wall, drew in deep breaths and gave vent to some silent oaths. As he calmed down, the sound of murmuring voices registered in his brain. In the lounge he could see the doc kneeling, gently applying iodine to Effie's bruised and scratched face. His housekeeper winced and the doc instantly apologised.

'So sorry. I'm being as careful as I can. We might see about a scan for that eye tomorrow.' Dr Simmonds sat back on her haunches and reached for another piece of clean cotton wool, dunked it in antiseptic. That's when she saw him, those blue pools blinking.

'No CT equipment on the island.' She wouldn't fit in if she was expecting fancy gear.

Her eyes widened, sending an odd thrill of excitement deep into his gut. 'Really? Then how do I find out what's going on with patients who need scans?'

'Serious cases are flown to Auckland. The rest are up to you.' Ben snapped his lips together. If she hadn't been informed about the basic facilities on the island, it wasn't his place to warn her. Hadn't Lissie told her the situation?

'Guess I'll have to adjust rather quickly to my new surroundings, then.' She didn't seem overly perturbed by his news, instead changing the subject. 'Did Riley settle all right?'

'Yes.' Out like a light.

'Thank you. It's been an exciting day for him, playing with his friends and going to the beach. He's exhausted.' She stifled a yawn and reached to wipe a blot of blood off Effie's chin.

'So are you.' The words were out of his mouth

before he'd barely thought them. Getting far too chatty with her. Time to get out of here. Go home and crack the top on an ice-cold beer.

Her hand stilled on Effie's arm. 'Nothing a good night's sleep won't fix.' She swallowed another yawn, shook her head as though refocusing. 'I'm about to clean and stitch these wounds now the local anaesthetic has started working.'

He didn't think. Instead he reacted. 'Want a hand?'

'What?' Astonishment lit up her face.

She looked delightful when she forgot to be resolute. 'I'll help.' Where had his brain gone tonight? Hadn't he already decided not to help her in any way, shape or form? Offering to assist in a medical situation was not a smart move. If he wasn't careful he'd be telling her his life story. But it was too late to back out. He'd say nothing and act like the cop he'd become. Dropping to his haunches, he pulled her bag towards him and took out some latex gloves that were in a pouch near the top.

Shoving his large hands into the small gloves

that barely covered his fingers, he grimaced. 'Should be safe to pass you things.'

The doc was still staring at him. 'I can manage.'

'Want needle and thread?'

Her sigh fell between them. She was about to argue. He could see the gathering words storming across her face. Then Effie groaned, and thankfully the doc's attention shifted to her patient.

He poked around in the kit for the cotton wool and antiseptic liquid, suddenly aware of the scent of lavender. Was that the doc's perfume?

'Thank you.' She whipped everything out of his fingers.

Ben found suture thread and the needle container. He snapped the plastic vial holding a single needle, pushed the end of the thread through the eyelet and handed it over to the doc. Then he watched as her long, elegant hands expertly pulled the two edges of the first, deeper wound together, stitching internally, then externally down Effie's leg.

'Want to give her a tetanus shot?' he asked thoughtlessly.

Those hands stilled for a brief moment. He'd gone too far. Now the questions really would start. He was way out of line, but the unexpected sense of ease that the familiar items in a simple medical bag gave him had made him careless with what he said.

The doc pulled the thread tight, tied off. 'Yes, Effie will need immunising when I've finished stitching.'

Silence fell in the room, broken only by his quiet search of the kit for the tetanus vial and a syringe, which took a while as he studied familiar tools and vials. Until now he'd have said he never missed his old career. Until now.

The doc asked, 'Effie, have you got someone to keep an eye on you overnight?'

Effie rolled her head to one side, winced with pain and whispered, 'My husband and my daughter are away.'

'Can she stay at your house?' Rachel asked him directly. 'She might be concussed.'

'In principle that would be fine, but Effie's a married woman, and people might get the wrong idea.' The islanders might misinterpret his motives. 'But she could stay with you.'

'Effie, would you be all right with staying with me here? I'm afraid I haven't got a spare bed yet.'

'That would be fine, Doctor.'

The doc stood, stretching up onto her toes as she arched her back. Her hands gripped her hips, and her breasts pushed the fabric of her skimpy blue singlet top upwards. Her slim thighs were taut under the knee-length shorts she wore.

Ben's mouth fell open. Snapped shut. Hell. He grappled for the very last threads of common sense still available in his skull. 'Thanks for everything, Doc. Effie, I hope you feel better soon.' And he almost ran for the front door and the familiar heavy night air where sanity prevailed.

CHAPTER TWO

RACHEL groaned and rolled over to see what the time was.

Four twenty-five. She gave another, louder groan. Those blasted roosters. Her head flopped back on the pillow and she absorbed all the foreign sounds of this tiny nation waking up. Birds she didn't recognise were also making their morning calls. An occasional motor scooter chugged past her front lawn. A cow mooed from somewhere on the hill behind the house.

She stretched and grinned. It was kind of exciting being in such a different environment. She couldn't be further from the chilly grey of London with the millions of people and the relentless traffic. And her parents. Her grin slipped.

Mum had been devastated when she'd heard Rachel's plans but had also been encouraging about taking a chance on a new life. If only Dad had shown signs of opening up to Riley she mightn't have come. But...she shrugged...dreams were free, and here she was, following one a very long way from her messed-up family.

Yesterday, as she'd watched Riley excitedly taking in the sights of odd-shaped trees with their green coconuts, the funny birds, the beach that followed them right around the island, she'd believed this had been the correct thing to do. On the day they'd arrived Riley had been tired and belligerent after the tedious hours spent in planes and airports. But yesterday he'd been full of beans, and paddling in the beautiful and safe lagoon had been a highlight for both of them.

Slipping out of bed, Rachel shrugged into a short satin robe and headed to the kitchen. A cup of tea on the tiny front deck while she watched the sun rise would be the perfect start to the day.

'Morning, Doctor,' Effie greeted her. 'You want a drink? I boiled the water for you.'

Startled, Rachel spun around. 'Effie. How's that head? And your thigh?' The colours from her bruises highlighting the little woman's face were impressive. 'I thought you'd still be asleep.'

'I'm always up early.' She held a cup out to Rachel. 'What do you like?'

'Tea, thank you, but you don't have to run around after me.'

'You fix my leg for me. Why don't I make your tea?'

How logical. 'Do you have children to get home to?'

Effie told her, 'My daughter, Nina, gets herself to school, but last night she stayed with a friend.' Effie's voice brightened. 'She's fourteen. After school she goes to the grocery shop to work.' She nodded through the window at the bungalow next door. 'I'll go to work for Ben this morning.'

Ben. Rachel turned to stare across the fence at the white bungalow with all its windows wide open. No need to lock up around here, Rachel mused. But, then, who would be game enough to take on such a big man as the local policeman, anyway?

Ben. A man of few words. Last night his abrupt

departure had annoyed her. The fact he hadn't made any mention of seeing her later rankled. She wanted to see him, get to know him a little better.

Thinking about her new neighbour made her tummy quiver as heat unfurled and unfamiliar desire rose. She'd tossed and turned half the night, wondering what it would be like to have him make love to her.

That body was something else. Jamie had also been a large man in superb physical condition so she knew exactly how those muscles would feel under her hands. Could imagine them rippling as her fingers slid over them. She blinked and turned back into the room.

'How long have you been keeping house for Ben?' she asked Effie.

'Since he came more than two years ago.' Effie giggled. 'He's messy. Clothes everywhere, plates and cups in the sink. Naughty man, I tell him, but he only laughs.'

So the man had flaws. Rachel grinned. Flaws were good, perfection was daunting. Then she had a brainwave. 'Do you want more work? I need someone to do my housework too. I'm only working nine to three most days unless there's an emergency, but I want to spend my free time with Riley, not on the end of a broom. At least until he's settled.'

Effie's face spread into a wide smile, lighting up the morning. 'I'd love to help you, Doctor. I can clean the house, do the washing and ironing, look after your little boy if you're late home. How many hours?'

Rachel smiled at Effie's enthusiasm. 'I don't know yet. Can I tell you later when I've got myself a little bit more sorted?' She would need to see how long it took her to get settled.

'Want me to help unpack all those boxes?'

'I'd love you to, but I still haven't decided where everything will go.' She'd had far too much furniture sent out.

'That's okay. You call me when you're ready. Ben will tell you where I live. Here's your tea.'

Rachel took the proffered cup. 'Thank you very

much. I'll take a look at your wounds before you leave.'

'Thanks, Doctor, but they'll be all right. I'm going next door now to make Ben his bacon and eggs. He gets up early too.'

Rachel pulled a chair out from the table. 'Ben can wait a few more minutes while I check you over.'

Effie laughed as she sat down. 'You're not as stern as you try to sound.'

'Must be losing my touch.' Rachel pulled on gloves then quickly tugged off the gauze covering Effie's wounds. 'Looking good. Don't get these wet, though. No shower, no swimming.'

Effie looked shocked. 'No shower?'

'Have a wash down.' Rachel tried to examine the bruised eye but gave up when Effie groaned. 'Sorry.'

'It's okay, Doctor.'

'You never said how you fell.'

'Skidded on the clean floor and banged into the glass door. Broke it, and hit my head on the corner of the bench on the way down.' Effie gave a rueful smile. 'Now I've got to go. That Ben needs feeding.'

Effie trotted down the path, favouring her injured leg, and ducked through the fence. Rachel suppressed the light envy that tripped through her. Effie was going to see Ben. And she wasn't.

What a darned shame. She couldn't think of a better way to start the day than rolling over in bed and finding Ben beside her. Which only went to show how much notice she took of her own warnings. Ben was out of bounds. Full stop. But he was a neighbour. She couldn't avoid him, didn't want to avoid him. But nothing. Ben was a handful of firm muscle, had a touch of arrogance, and, if the way he'd seen to Effie last night was anything to go by, he was someone who'd definitely put himself out there to care for others. Which made him a hero of sorts.

And she would never, ever go near a hero kind of guy again. Since when had she got over Jamie's death enough to even be thinking about another man? The shock of losing her husband so suddenly still woke her at the deepest part of the night, sometimes with tears saturating her pillow. Her anger at Jamie was real but she missed him terribly. She wasn't ready to move on. She might never be. The thought of suffering that kind of pain and grief again had so far stopped her wanting to get involved with another man.

What about having an affair? With someone as scorching hot as Ben? Her eyes drifted to Ben's house. It would be so easy. Too easy. Until it was over and then what? Every morning she'd sit out on her deck and he'd be just over the fence. She'd be straining her ears to hear the slightest sound, be watching furtively for a glimpse of him. The island was too small to avoid anyone for very long. Life would be difficult if not impossible because she wasn't the kind of woman to have a fling and walk away. Even in a brief, totally sexual encounter she gave too much of herself, needed too much back. She didn't do sex for the sake of it. She'd tried it once while at university and had got burnt—nobody's fault but her own. So, no fling with her neighbour.

Disappointment tugged her shoulders down.

Tipping the tea away, Rachel concentrated on making another cup, this time black.

Three hours later Rachel had Riley dressed, breakfasted, and ready to start out on their first proper day in the islands. The rest of the unpacking would have to wait.

'Need a lift?' The deep, gruff voice of last night's dreams broke through her thoughts from her back door.

Stomping down on a sudden burst of excitement, Rachel reluctantly told Ben, 'Thanks, but we're catching the bus.'

Hot damn. He looked good in his freshly pressed uniform. The light blue of his shirt accentuated the black of his eyes and hair. His biceps filled the sleeves in a mouthwatering way. The black trousers fitted perfectly. He had a body to die for. She grinned. She'd been doing a lot of that since arriving here. But who could blame her? Then Ben's left eyebrow rose and she switched the grin off.

Riley slowly approached, shy of Ben today. 'You read me a story last night.'

Ben bent down to his level. 'Hey, kid, good morning.'

Those trousers stretching across Ben's butt accentuated the very tidy shape. A shape she'd love to cup with her hands, to feel his hot flesh against her palms. Rachel closed her eyes briefly. To stop herself staring. To prevent Ben seeing the lust she knew would be gleaming there. To get herself back under control. What was wrong with her this morning? One glimpse of a man in a uniform and she was having X-rated thoughts. Oh, no. She wasn't a uniform follower, surely? Jamie had always looked dashing in his and she'd loved ogling him. Clearly it was the uniform and not Ben that had her in such a stew. Thank goodness she'd said no to the ride.

But Riley wrecked everything by suddenly opening up to Ben, a big, peanut-butter-smeared smile on his face. 'Can I have a ride with you in the police truck? Can we have the lights flashing?'

Ben looked bamboozled at the onslaught. 'No lights.'

Rachel reacted without thought. 'No, Riley. You're not racing around the island in a police car. Taking a ride with Ben is one thing but I'll not have you thinking you're playing cops with him.' Her son was *not* going to be a policeman. He would grow up with a balanced outlook on helping people. He would not think he had to rush in fearlessly to save people while putting himself in danger at the same time.

'All boys want to be a policeman or fireman. It goes with the genes.'

Obviously she was meant to take him seriously. 'Not my boy.'

'Your call.' Ben shrugged eloquently, letting her know he didn't agree. Too bad. Riley was her responsibility.

Riley looked from Rachel to Ben and back. Then an abrupt subject change. 'I'm going to play with Harry today.'

Rachel's throat blocked. Riley had turned to Ben as though it was the most natural thing in the world. Which it definitely was not for her sad little boy. But for some inexplicable reason

Ben seemed to touch a chord with Riley that no other man had since Jamie's death. Because Ben didn't try too hard? Fear gripped her. Was this a good idea? What if Riley got too close to him? It would break his little heart all over again when they moved on. This wasn't a permanent destination for them. At least she hadn't planned on it being so.

Ben glanced at her. 'I'm leaving in five.'

Yes, so? 'We're going to the hospital.'

'I go past the front door.'

The main road did not go that close to the hospital. But it would be easier to catch a ride with Ben and not have to walk up the hill to the hospital with her bag while towing Riley along as well. 'Then thank you, I accept.'

'Okay.'

'Can I throw a box of medical books in your vehicle?'

'No problem.' He headed back down the path.

Rachel stared at his departing back. That's it? The man had no conversational skills whatsoever.

Or was that something he'd deliberately culti-
vated to keep people at bay? If so, why?

Come to think about it, why was someone as
obviously bright and ambitious as Ben living in
Rarotonga? She had nothing against Rarotonga,
but she couldn't imagine that the police department in a community this size had a lot of
complex cases for him to sink his teeth into.
Something about this scenario did not ring true.

*But, hey, look who's talking? You're here, aren't
you?* Lissie may have sweet-talked her into giving it a try, but she hadn't come here because she
couldn't keep up with the best of them back in
London. And she definitely wasn't going backwards by working for a small country. If anything, her qualifications would be enhanced with
the women's clinic she was setting up.

So she had no place speculating on Ben's reasons for being here. But she was interested in
him and wanted to know what made him tick.
Her mouth twitched as she fought a grin. A perfect excuse to be nosy. Better be a little cautious,
though. He might bite. Now, there was a thought.

Her skin cells danced in happy anticipation even though that wasn't going to happen.

Ben carried the doc's box of books into her office while she jabbered on with the woman who'd taken up the post as the doc's secretary, Colleen. In her fifties, Colleen and her husband, Ed, had moved over from Wellington for the warmer climate in the hope it would ease Ed's arthritis. According to Lissie, Colleen was efficiency personified, and would have the doc so organised the only thing she'd have to do on her own was breathe.

A huge vase of red-and-yellow hibiscus blooms sat in the centre of the desk. New pens and a large pad had been lined up neatly. The doc probably wouldn't realise how much she was wanted and needed here.

'Wow, are those for me? What a lovely surprise.' Rachel spoke up behind him, making him start. Brushing past him, her arm slid across his and he had to fight the urge to haul her against him. Imagine if he did. There'd be fireworks for sure.

'They're all yours,' he croaked.

'Makes me feel very special.'

'Watch out for ants.' When her exquisitely styled eyebrows arched at him, Ben added, 'Off the flowers.'

She placed her medical bag on the desk.

His warning obviously hadn't sunk in. 'Your bag. Ants.'

Her pale face turned a dusky pink. 'Okay, slow learner.' Her bow-shaped mouth curved into a sweet smile that twisted his belly and flooded him with warmth. Rachel's glance checked the empty shelves, the hospital bed pushed against one wall, and she chuckled. 'Well, here we go. First day of my new job. It's quite exciting to be practising in such a different environment.'

'It won't be easy.' In case she'd missed the point last night, she needed to be warned that there'd be no fancy diagnostic equipment, should be told that second opinions came via the phone or email. At the end of the day the buck stopped with her. There were going to be times when she'd feel very isolated. How she dealt with that would be a test of her mettle. Somehow Ben didn't think she'd be found wanting. But he was only guessing. Her needlework last night had been fine, but that had a degree of difficulty of one on a scale of one to ten.

'There'll probably be moments when I'll wish I was back in London, but right now I see this as a challenge. It's all too easy to take everything for granted when you work in a very modern hospital with all the equipment and staff you need available at the push of a button.'

Should he tell her he'd happily discuss any diagnosis problems she might have? Icy bumps lifted the skin on his arms. No way could he do that. Not now, not ever. What was happening to him that he'd even consider such a thing?

'Ben, Rachel, there you are.' Lissie bounced into the room, her smile wide, her eyes filled with happiness. 'Glad you brought Rachel in, Ben. I ran out of time with Jason arguing that he shouldn't go to school when Harry and Riley didn't have to.' Lissie wrapped her arms around the doc in a big hug. Rachel seemed to sink into her friend's arms as though she needed the comfort.

'Not a problem,' he muttered.

Lissie dropped her arms, turning to him. 'I hear poor Effie was our new doctor's first patient after her accident last night.'

'Right.' Ben watched the ease the women had with one another. A sense of loss, of being on the outside, slammed into him. When had been the last time someone had hugged him? As in an affectionate kind of hug? Far too long ago. Since when had he even needed a damned hug? Right now, as it happened. After last night's onslaught of emotions over Catrina, he'd ached with need for closeness to someone. Quickly, before he let despair take hold, he dug deep for the strength to haul up the protective barrier he usually kept wrapped around his heart and soul. He didn't need close friends. He was a stand-alone man these days. Far safer. For them, as well as him.

'How did you hear about Effie?' Rachel grinned at the other doctor.

'Everyone knows everything that goes on in

Raro. Don't forget that if you decide to do something you don't want found out.' Lissie grinned back. 'Colleen has taken Riley for a look at the carp in the pond outside. She's happy to look after him until Lanette gets here to collect him. Lanette's running a bit late.'

The doc shrugged and laughed again. 'So Riley's not a problem? He can sit in here with me until your sister-in-law turns up.'

'Colleen will be spoiling him rotten already. She loves kids, and misses her grandkids heaps.'

Ben straightened up from leaning against the wall. 'I'm off. I can drop Riley at Lanette's.'

The doc's mouth tightened. 'I thought you were on your way to work.'

Didn't she like him stepping in to help? 'I go past Lanette's house.'

'Okay, then, thanks. I'll come and find him, explain the change of plan.' Her mouth eased off the tension.

Lissie asked, 'Ben, do you know anyone with a reliable car for sale? Rachel's adamant she needs one, though I keep telling her the buses are fine.'

'I don't fancy catching a bus hauling a week's worth of groceries with me.' Rachel sighed. 'Besides, what happens if I get called in during the night? No buses then.'

'Use my car.' The offer was out before Ben had thought through the ramifications. 'Until I find you one to buy.'

'Won't you need it?' the doc asked.

'Got a work truck.'

Lissie explained, 'The cops are allowed to use their vehicles to go to and from work, which means they can stop just about anywhere in their own time.' She looked at her watch. 'Rachel, you've got lots of people waiting to meet you before your first clinic at ten.'

'Right, I'll say goodbye to Riley and get started.'

Ben stepped out of the office. Time to put some miles between him and his distracting neighbour. Distracting? An exploding petrol tanker would be a distraction. This woman made much more of an impact. He should never have hung around in her office, but he'd wanted to see her in her working space so he could picture her throughout his day. He had a sense of losing control, of acting like a lovesick puppy around her.

He suspected she'd be a superb obstetrician. Ask him to justify that and he couldn't, but Rachel had a purposeful air that demanded confidence in her. The women had been talking for weeks now about the new ladies' doctor coming to the island. One of his colleagues said his wife would've gone back to New Zealand to have her baby if the doc hadn't been appointed. He believed the women were in good hands.

Stepping outside, Ben shook away the old, familiar hospital smells that had taunted him while he'd been inside. Formalin seemed to have a way of getting into everything, even in rooms where it was never used. It had a smell most people disliked but he'd accepted it as part of his life a very long time ago when he'd started his medical training.

He strode away, swearing under his breath. He did not need this. It was all the doc's fault these once-buried memories were pounding at him again. Why couldn't Lissie have found her a house to rent further around the island, closer to the hospital? Why did he keep opening his trap and offering to do things for her? Like taking the kid to Lanette's. That need to help her he'd felt last night would not go away.

Ben headed to the pond and slapped his hands on his hips as he watched the boy leaning over the water, following a large carp swimming around the edge. Beside him the doc was talking softly, her face full of love.

Stay away from the kid, Ben growled to himself as his heart rolled over. Stay away from the doc, he hissed in his mind as his stomach tightened. Then life would return to its uneasy but uneventful pace and he could slip back into obscurity.

Rachel followed Colleen through the hospital, being stopped every few minutes by someone wanting to shake her hand and welcome her to Rarotonga. 'I'm starting to feel like royalty,' she quipped to Colleen. 'I only hope I can remember everyone's names.'

'You'll be fine.' Colleen stopped at the open door to the maternity ward. 'At least this should look familiar to you.'

Stepping into the noisy room with windows pushed open to allow in any breeze that might come this way, Rachel paused to assimilate the atmosphere. There was something special about maternity wards. She supposed it was because of the excitement for the new lives. Expectant mums and those who'd already delivered stopped chattering and watched her, their faces open and friendly.

'Hello, I'm Dr Rachel Simmonds.'

They swarmed her, two young women bringing their newborn babes for her to inspect. Rachel took each in turn to cuddle. Babies—who could resist them?

Then a stunningly beautiful woman approached and spoke in a soft lilt. 'Hello, I'm Manea, the midwife.' After giving Rachel a welcoming embrace she said, 'I'd like to talk to you about one of my patients.'

In the little office off to the side of the ward

Rachel listened while Manea explained her patient's symptoms. 'Kiriana is having her first baby at age thirty-five, which is very late for an islander. She's been on the internet reading up about everything that can go wrong. And now she wants a whole battery of tests done that I can't provide.'

'This is when I dislike the net intensely. All it achieves is to cause more worry than a pregnant woman should have.' Rachel read Kiriana's notes. 'Everything seems perfectly normal. No anaemia, no hepatitis, blood pressure's good.'

'Could you examine her?' Manea asked. 'It might settle her down to have a doctor taking her fears seriously. I'm the girl who grew up next door. Not likely to be totally convincing when it comes to persuading her everything's going well.'

'Can you arrange an appointment for her? Might as well see her as soon as possible. She hasn't mentioned amniocentesis?'

'Down's syndrome is top of her list for things that can go wrong.'

'It would be.' Rachel sighed. People put themselves through untold worry at times. 'I'll see her as soon as she can come in.'

They went on to discuss all Manea's patients but the midwife had no other concerns. 'Hopefully I won't be bothering you too often,' she said as she put the patient notes away in a filing cabinet. 'But I'm thrilled to have an obstetrician to be able to call on if necessary. I bet the GPs are pleased too.'

'I haven't met them yet. I'll drop into the medical centre some time over the next few days to make myself known.'

Colleen piped up. 'All sorted. You're to go on Thursday afternoon.'

Rachel started. 'Thanks for that.'

Colleen glanced at her watch. 'Right now you've got a patient waiting to see you.'

'Already?' They certainly weren't giving her time to settle in.

'It's a straightforward consult. One of the bosses at the airline's office wants to meet you just in case anything goes wrong with her pregnancy. She's flying home to Auckland next month, four weeks before her baby is due, but is playing it safe.' Colleen smiled cautiously. 'I think you'll get a lot of that—playing safe. Especially with the Kiwis.'

'That's fine. Understandable, I suppose, if they're used to big, modern hospitals.' Rachel shrugged away her disappointment. She liked to see a pregnancy through to the end, not be a stopgap measure. But who could blame women who wanted to go home to be with family and friends when they were having a baby?

The day of Riley's birth was still vivid in her mind. She'd been in awe of the tiny bundle the midwife had handed her. And the stunned expression on Jamie's face and the unqualified love in his eyes as he'd met his son for the very first time had taken her breath away. There'd been a steady stream of friends and colleagues visiting her and Riley while she'd remained in hospital. And Jamie had hardly left her side until he'd been able to take them home.

So why had Jamie gone and got himself shot?

What had possessed him to do something so stupid he'd deprived Riley of his father?

She felt tears welling up in her eyes. Nearly two years later and she still couldn't fathom Jamie's actions that day. She was still angry and hurt. Pulling herself together for the people who needed her to be strong, she blindly followed Colleen down the corridor. Bring on the work, the patients, the mind-diverting everyday things that would get her past these moments.

The work would settle her, help ease the pain of the past and, just maybe, make the future a little more appealing than it had been since Jamie's murder.

CHAPTER THREE

RACHEL saw her patient out and turned back to her office. After only a few days she felt completely at home in this small hospital.

'Doc, how's your morning been?' Ben's voice reached her from across the hall, caressed her skin, turning the humid heat to a dry sizzle.

She whipped around, hoping he put her red cheeks down to her not being used to working in temperatures in the high twenties. 'Ben. What are you doing here? I thought you were on duty today.'

'I've brought someone in for urgent medical attention.' His gaze cruised over her face, down her neck and on down her body as he lounged against the wall.

The sizzle became sparks. Forget high twenties, try high thirties. The air-conditioning was next to useless so earlier she'd thrown open all the windows, but right now she was overcooking.

His gaze had stuck on her legs. She shouldn't have worn a short skirt to work but most of her clothes were not suitable for this climate. The skirt should've been cool but she might as well be wearing woollen trousers for all the good it did. Ben had an unprecedented effect on her. A lingering glance from him and she had all the backbone of one of those jellyfish purported to be beyond the reef. What would it be like to succumb to that provocative sensuality glittering out at her?

Closing her eyes, she breathed deeply. Whatever the answer, she was not about to find out. Concentrate. And not on what he seemed to be thinking either. 'What's the problem with the patient?'

'He's got too much spare time on his hands.'

'What's wrong medically?'

Ben grimaced. 'He fell while climbing out of his truck outside the police station, knocked himself unconscious on the kerb. He had a fit and nearly swallowed his tongue but we managed to prevent that.'

'We?'

'Okay, me.' Ben shrugged.

'He's a very lucky man.' Lucky Ben knew what to do in the circumstances. Another example of his competence around injured folk. Had he done a first-aid course? Probably a prerequisite to being a policeman here. 'What about the head wound? Is he going to be all right?'

'Lissie's with him. He's got a hard head.'

Rachel raised her eyebrows. Surely he was joking? A tiny glint twinkled back at her from those intense black eyes. So he was teasing. Who'd have believed it? The man had a fun side after all.

'Glad to hear he'll be all right.' She paused. 'While you're here, are you sure you're happy with me giving Effie some extra work?' Why had she asked? To make polite conversation? Not likely. Shock rippled through her. She was trying to delay him, keep him talking to her. It didn't matter what about; she just wanted to watch the lines of his face when he spoke. He had a strong face that softened when he thought no one was looking. His mouth could be grim, as it had been when he'd delivered Effie to her, but it could also lift into the most stomach-crunching, heart-melting smile that made her think of the sun coming out behind the grey snow clouds on an English winter's day.

'No problem. Got time for a coffee?' he muttered, then looked distinctly uncomfortable.

Regretting his invitation already? 'Yes, I do, as it happens.' Clinic didn't start for another twenty minutes.

'Oh, right.'

'Where do we go? I haven't found out what's available here. Colleen always appears with coffee just as I start to feel in need of caffeine.' A mischievous impulse made her step in front of him and look up into his eyes. The mischief faded as those eyes widened and something like desire danced through them. The emotion she could read in Ben's face was rolling through her own body at the steady, unrelenting pace of a juggernaut. Intense, persistent and so exciting. As though Ben had flicked on a hundred switches all over her body and flooded her with such warmth that she was melting.

And he hadn't even touched her, not with so much as one fingertip.

This need hit her hard. It had been a long time since she'd wanted a man. A long time since she'd last made love. To Jamie. A cooling breeze brushed over her skin. Or was it a dose of reality? Jamie. Her one true love. The man she'd thought she'd be spending the rest of her life with, having more children with. A shiver shimmied up her spine and she rubbed her hands down her arms, felt the goose-bumps under her palms. Lusting after Ben was a mistake; following up on it would be disastrous. She took a backward step, away from Ben, away from temptation.

Ben's gaze darkened. Not used to being walked away from? They were in for some difficult times if they didn't get this sorted and the attraction put in perspective before it erupted into something neither of them could control.

Rachel drew a shaky breath, steeled her shoulders, and said, 'Come to think of it, I should probably go over to the clinic early.'

'Right.' His eyes bored into her. Was he sorry? Relieved? Who would know? He wasn't exactly a bag of information, didn't seem to see the need to let people in on his feelings.

'Ben, we seem to have got off on the wrong foot. I really don't want to get involved with anyone, whether for one night or a month. I'm still coming to terms with losing my husband. It's like I'm riding a roller-coaster. One day I think I'm moving on, getting a new life; the next it's as though I'm still back at that first day, hearing the chief constable telling me Jamie wouldn't be coming home ever again. It's been hard. I still miss him.'

She stopped. What on earth was she doing, telling him all this? He didn't need to know. A simple 'No, thank you' to that desire lurking in his eyes would've been enough. But she wanted him so badly it hurt. She yearned to be held by those strong arms, to be taken away on a wave of passion so wild that she forgot everything for a short while. She stared up at the man who'd unlocked this need in her. 'I'm sorry.'

Now he did touch her. A gentle trace down her cheek with his forefinger. 'Don't be. I understand.'

Really? 'Thanks.'

'My wife died nearly three years ago.' Pain bleached his suntanned cheeks, cracked his voice, shook the finger on her cheek. 'I miss her every minute of every day.'

Then he was gone. Striding down the corridor as though the devil was after him, sending him on his way— away from her. Leaving her to contemplate the coincidence that they'd both lost a spouse. He really did understand her mixed-up emotions.

Ben slammed the truck door shut, snapped the ignition key on, and clanged the shift into forward drive.

Then hesitated. Rachel reminded him of things he'd banned from his life for ever. Essential things like caring for someone special, like sharing day-to-day occurrences such as buying the milk, cleaning the kitchen bench after having a meal together.

His head banged back against the headrest. He had told her about Catrina. He never talked about his late wife. To anyone. Not to his friends. Not to his family. No one. Yet he'd blurted it out to the doc whom he'd known less than a week. The shock in her eyes had woken him up from that desire-induced state he'd slipped into. Desire had crept through him without thought, without any hindrance on his part, igniting a deep need he hadn't known he had. A need to love again, to be loved again. How had this happened? All he'd done was ask her if she wanted a coffee.

All he'd done?

When was the last time he'd asked a woman out for a coffee?

You invited Catrina to join you at that café down on the wharf in Wellington. You'd been watching her feeding the pigeons and fallen in love with her there and then. You walked right up to her, introduced yourself and offered to buy her a cappuccino. Yes, she'd said so fast you'd had to check you'd heard her correctly. She'd grinned. And the rest was history.

Except it had been a short history. Catrina's life had been cut off when she'd overshot the motorway off-ramp, made an abrupt turn at speed and lost control of the car. Life was cruel. While he hadn't got much more than a scratch, Catrina's ribcage had been crushed by the steering wheel. Flail chest. Every time she'd breathed those broken ribs had torn at her lungs.

All his medical training had been for nothing that night. The best he'd been able to do had been to hold Catrina's hand and talk to her as they waited for the paramedics—who were never going to be able to save her. He hadn't been able to save her life, or even dull her pain. He'd been useless. Devastated as he'd watched the life leave his beautiful, vibrant Catrina. Furious that he'd felt relief when she could no longer feel the excruciating pain.

Ben gasped a lungful of humid air. He eased his foot onto the accelerator and drove carefully down the narrow lane out to the main route into town. His hands were shaking. Sweat beaded on his brow. He hadn't consciously thought about that night in months. He didn't go there any more than necessary. It hurt too much. That night had been the end of one life and the start of another less involved one that had brought him here, away from family and friends. His wife was squeezed into a tight, locked cell in his heart, only to be taken out when he got so desperate for her laughter, her wisdom, her chatter that he couldn't ignore it. And every time he did that he sank into a black hole that took a binge session at the pub to blot out the pain.

So why had he lifted the lid on all that now? Why with Rachel Simmonds? The doc. Something about her had touched him in a place he'd long believed dried up and dead. It wasn't sex. Oh, he wanted that as well. No doubt about it. But that wasn't what was going on here. So what was? He didn't have an answer.

You don't want an answer. You're too afraid of where it will take you.

The truck surged forward as Ben's foot pressed the accelerator. His shoulders bit into the seat behind him. *Whoa, slow down, man.*

Slow down on everything. Especially slow down on being friendly with your new neighbour.

Take every day one moment at a time. Stay as far away from her as you possibly can. Give her time to settle in. Get to know her slowly. Why? Because then you'll have got past this wish to make love to her, to look out for her, to show her how things work in island life, and then you'll be able to have a normal, friendly, neighbourly relationship with her.

Ben grunted. One day at a time? Sure. He could do that. If he was blind and deaf. If his peanut brain returned to normal.

Rachel flopped down on the towel she'd spread over the sand. Splashing around in the sea was the perfect way to finish a day after work. Not that work had been strenuous, far from it. Evcryone she met, staff and patients, were very friendly. She might find her enjoyment from the job again if this kept up. But from her life? That was expecting too much.

The sound of clapping came from further down the beach where a wedding was taking place. The bride looked gorgeous in her cream-and-gold dress as her new husband kissed her. Her attendants wore gold, strapless gowns, while the men were dressed in open-necked cream shirts, tan trousers and bare feet. Rachel grinned. Back home no one would believe her when she told them. Bare feet at a wedding? Practical in the sand and a fun element in the photos. The clear sky and blue waters of the lagoon made a perfect setting for the ceremony. No wonder so many Kiwis came over here to get married.

'Mummy, look at me jumping the waves,' Riley called from the water's edge where tiny wavelets lapped.

'Watch out for sharp rocks,' she called back. A cut on his foot could take some time to heal in this moist heat.

'He loves the beach.' Ben hunkered down on his haunches beside her.

She swallowed. With the effect Ben had on her she should've sensed him coming. It had taken time and a patient in labour for her to get past his startling revelation that morning. Then there was the way her body had reacted to him. That had taken longer to get over, and by the tingling in her fingertips and in her tummy now she hadn't been very successful.

But she did understand some of Ben's reticence when it came to opening up and talking. Which only made what he'd told her even more surprising. Why had he told her? Was it because she'd been so open about her feelings surrounding Jamie's death? Well, there were a few things she hadn't mentioned and had no intention of telling him any time in the near future. Things best kept to herself.

'Can he swim?' Ben's gaze was firmly fixed on Riley.

'No. Last weekend was the first time he'd been to a beach.'

'I'll teach him.'

'What?' Ben offering to show Riley how to

swim would mean several visits to the beach, would mean he'd be spending more time with them.

'He needs to know. To be safe.'

'I realise that. I'm going to enrol him for lessons as soon as I find out more about them.'

At last Ben turned to her. The passion of that morning was no longer visible in his eyes. Instead his look was guarded. Unexpectedly that hurt her deeply. Surely he didn't think she was going to broach the subject of his wife every time she saw him?

But all he said was 'You won't find a swimming class as such anywhere on the island. Local kids learn to swim almost before they start to walk. The lagoon is relatively safe, but Riley still needs to know how to swim as well as the kids he'll be playing with. They'll forget he isn't as competent as them and won't think to look out for him. If he's like most boys I know, he'll want to do everything they do, which includes diving and snorkelling. I can start showing him right now. He'll be swimming like a fish in no time at all.'

Rachel smothered a smile. Ben mightn't talk a lot but occasionally he made up for it. He was relentless when it came to getting what he wanted. 'Thank you. I accept your generous offer.'

'Not generous, sensible.' His gaze returned to Riley, who'd now spotted Ben and was racing up the sand towards them.

'Hello, Ben. Did you see me in the water?'

'Sure did, kid.'

Why did he always call Riley 'kid'? And, for that matter, why did he always call her 'Doc'? She'd heard him call locals by their names so it was only with her and Riley he did this. Keeping *them* specifically at arm's length?

He turned to her as he stood up. 'What about you? Can you swim?'

'No. But I'm not going to be diving and snorkelling.'

'I'll teach you too.' He held his hand out to her. 'Starting now.'

She stared at the proffered hand. So strong and big, calloused from outdoor work. She could trust a man with hands like Ben's. She could let him nearer than she'd let anyone since Jamie. Slowly she placed her hand in his. And was wrenched to her feet. Looking into his eyes, she saw the same sudden regret she'd seen that morning. Had he changed his mind? Disappointment racked her. A moment ago she hadn't wanted to have him teach her; now she'd do almost anything for him to step into the sea with her and show her how to be safe there.

'Let's go,' he muttered, before charging down the beach, still holding her hand and tugging her along.

'Let's start with learning to float.' Ben lifted Riley off his feet and laid him on his back on top of the water, keeping his hands under the kid's body as reassurance. 'See, it's easy. You try, Doc.'

Her face screwed into a grimace. She gulped and sank down on her knees, the water lapping her chin.

She looked cute, but there was worry in those eyes staring back at him. 'Just lie on your back, keeping your body straight. Try not to sag at your waist.' He glanced at her waist. Big mistake. A diamond stud in her belly button winked at him. His mouth dried. Today he'd made more mistakes with this woman than he'd made with a string of one-night stands in the past three years. Why hadn't she worn a long shirt and a pair of knee-length shorts instead of that skimpy, bluebell-coloured bikini?

'I'm doing it, Mummy. Look at me.'

The doc immediately stood up to study her boy. 'So you are, clever clogs.'

'You can do it too, Mummy. Ben will hold you. I don't need him now.'

Hell, kid. Shut your mouth. You don't know what you're suggesting here. Ben watched the doc's face turn an endearing shade of red and was grateful for his tan as he felt his own skin warming.

'I think you should learn first. I'll try another day.' She didn't look Ben in the eye as she started past him.

'Coward,' he whispered.

Her head flung up, her eyes spitting at him. 'Never.'

'Lie on your back, then.' Hopefully she'd ignore him and continue back to the beach. Bet she wouldn't. Not the Rachel he'd seen so far, anyway. She took challenges on the chin, like when he'd turned up, a complete stranger with a bleeding woman in his arms, and had all but forced his way into her house.

Rachel glared at him.

Darn, now he was calling her Rachel. But when confronted by an annoyed goddess with sparks coming from her fierce blue eyes, with that fair hair falling over her flawless skin, what hope did he have of keeping his distance? *And* she was dressed in scraps of fabric about the size of his hands. Hands. Touching her skin. Everywhere. His hormones rampaged out of control. Swallow. Get the hell off the beach.

Rachel slid down into the water and lay on her back.

Ben gawped like a teenager as those scantily clad breasts pointed skywards. As she struggled to stay afloat she pushed her hips up and her waist dipped into the sea. Instinctively he placed a hand on the small of her back and pushed up. 'Keep your back straight.'

The sea made her skin slick, soft under his palm. When she wriggled and tried to straighten up, hot, hard need stabbed him like a punch in the gut. He dropped his hand, stepped away. Sank into the water on his haunches, aware of the shape the front of his shorts had taken on.

Lesson one. Don't touch the pupil. At least, not this one.

Lesson two. Find someone else to teach the doc to swim.

Riley sidled closer to him, bobbing in the slightly deeper water, totally unfazed at being out of his depth, totally trusting Ben to be there for him. 'Hey, Ben, can I learn to float on my tummy now?'

Grateful for the interruption, Ben focused entirely on the kid. 'Absolutely.' He held Riley in his hands and showed him how to hold his head out of the water and how to kick so he could move along.

When Rachel headed back to the beach Ben pretended not to notice. No way was he going to watch that sassy backside all the way to her towel. He'd be staying in the water half the night if he did.

Riley had barely finished his dinner before he fell asleep, as had been the case every night since his first swimming lesson with Ben three days ago.

Tucking him into bed, Rachel smiled tenderly, her heart squeezing. 'You've never been so busy, had so much excitement. Soon you'll be racing around like a local: swimming, climbing palm trees, fishing off the rocks.'

If for no other reason than having Riley happy, this move had been the best thing she'd done. And if Riley could find such happiness here then maybe she could too.

Lissie was helping her settle in. Her friend was different here, much more relaxed and happy. She had time for her kids too, something that had always been lacking back in London. She was making Rachel's life easier by introducing her to family and friends, by ensuring she had everything she needed. Bottom line, Lissie didn't want her leaving and would do everything in her power to keep her here. Even find her a husband if she had her own way.

Then there was Effie. The tiny woman had more energy than two other people put together. She kept Rachel's house spotless and the laundry done almost before they stepped out of their clothes. The only job Rachel didn't hand over was cooking their meals. Cooking wasn't Effie's forte and the plain, local food didn't suit Rachel's palate. But otherwise it was a match made in heaven. A little decadent, maybe, but it freed her up to spend lots of time with Riley.

Rachel took a cold lemonade out onto the deck and sat watching the sunset. Brilliant shades of orange and red seared the sky, and pink tones filtered around the edges where sky met sea. Beautiful, stunning. She sipped her drink and leaned back against the railing pole. This was her favourite hour of the day. No demands on her time. No need to do anything but relax. Face it, there wasn't much to do even if she'd wanted to. Island life was simple and wonderful.

The ringing of the phone shattered the moment. It had to be Lissie. No one else would be calling her. But when she answered she heard the worried voice of Manea. 'Can you come to the hospital and see my patient? We've got a breech birth on our hands.'

Rachel put the phone down and flicked on some lights. Riley wasn't going to be happy about getting dragged out of bed, but she had no choice. Or did she? There was a light on next door so Ben must be at home. Could she ask him to keep an eye on Riley for her? She didn't want to. He might consider her to be taking advantage of him when he was already doing so much for them.

Thinking of how exhausted Riley had been, Rachel bit down on a sigh. She'd ask Ben this once, and tomorrow she'd set about finding someone to be available to babysit when these situations arose. Effie had offered but she had her own family to look after.

Slipping through the fence, Rachel made her way to Ben's porch and nearly leapt out of her skin when he spoke from the darkness.

'Hello, there.'

'Hell, you gave me a fright.' She paused, steadied her breathing, waiting for her heart rate to return to normal. 'I'm sorry to bother you, but I've been called in to the hospital. There's a breech birth.'

'Take the car.'

'Yes, thanks. But I've got a problem. Riley's sound asleep and I don't really want to get him up.' She winced and waited to be told to go away. Or, worse, hear resignation in his voice as he offered to keep an eye on the kid.

'Your deck's as comfortable as mine.' He sounded totally unfazed that she'd asked a favour of him.

'I didn't expect to need a sitter so soon. Should've known better. I am in the business of babies and they don't take the slightest bit of notice about who they might be inconveniencing when they're ready to come out.'

'Any time you're stuck, call me.' He stood up, looming out of the dark. 'Effie's got a teenage niece, Molly, very responsible, works at the pharmacy. You might want to talk to her.'

Smiling, Rachel shook her head. 'Is there anyone or anything you don't know?'

'Not really. Comes with the territory of being a cop in a small population.' He stepped down beside her. 'Though I'm still trying to fathom my new neighbour.'

Ben had no need to check on Riley after the first time. The kid was sound asleep, his teddy bear in a vice-like grip at his throat. But for the third time in an hour Ben stood in the bedroom doorway and watched the deep, unconcerned breathing of an exhausted little boy.

What was it like to have a child of your own? Definitely scary. There were so many things that could go wrong. He'd be permanently worried if he was a dad. But there was that something special he saw on the doc's face whenever she watched her son. A tender love that knew no bounds. A mother's unconditional love. Did a father's love feel like that? He couldn't imagine why it wouldn't. To have his child at his side, teaching him or her to swim, to climb trees, to play with them, hug them when they were unhappy—these were things Ben tried not to imagine.

A photo frame stood on the bedside table. Ben stepped into the bedroom and picked it up, took it out to the light in the hall. A man held Riley in his arms. Had to be the kid's dad. The two shared the same green eyes, the same generous mouth. There was love in the guy's eyes as he smiled at his boy. Riley must miss him a lot. What boy wouldn't? It was absolutely tragic that he'd lost his dad so young.

His gaze strayed to Rachel standing beside the man, her face beaming at the camera, her eyes sparkling happily. She looked completely relaxed. No shadows marred her face, no tension in her stance, or sadness in her eyes. A Rachel he hadn't seen yet.

Quietly Ben replaced the photo. He and Catrina had wanted to wait to have children. They'd wanted to establish themselves in their careers, buy a house, and generally set themselves up for a comfortable life first. Seemed silly now. But back then they'd believed they'd had all the time in the world to accomplish their goals.

Not that kids were goals, necessarily. Giving them a good life was—but having them should be a natural progression of falling in love and marrying. And if they hadn't put having a family on hold, he might now be a parent, have a part of Catrina with him.

Ben spun around, headed down the hall. The kid didn't need watching over. And *he* didn't need to be standing looking at someone else's child as though Riley could fill the void in his heart.

At the lounge doorway he paused and peered in. The doc had finished unpacking most of her boxes. There were pictures on the walls now. Interested to see what appealed to her, he flicked a switch and the room lit up brightly.

Colourful, vibrant abstracts covered one wall, demanding attention with their bold lines. Ben studied each of the paintings and decided he liked them all. The doc had good taste. He grinned at his arrogance. The doc had good taste because he agreed with her?

'Yep.' He headed out to the deck and the cooler night air. He needed something to chill down these crazy thoughts spinning relentlessly in his head. Kids. The doc's taste in art. What else did they have in common? Medicine, for starters… but Rachel was the doctor around here, not him. He swallowed that sour taste. Okay, what else? They both liked to spend time in the sea. Tame, Ben, tame. *What you're really getting around to is the fact that you fancy her and she fancies you right back.*

And just like that, he was hot. Hot and hard. And she wasn't even in sight, let alone anywhere near. Rachel repeatedly did this to him. In bed at night—alone—he'd fantasise about making love to her. During the late afternoons when he was teaching her how to swim he had to fight hard not to drag her into his arms and kiss her senseless. Early mornings when she sat out here, having her tea, he'd catch glimpses of her as he moved about his house, and he'd want to come over and kiss her good morning.

The only cure, very temporary at that, was to run down the beach and dive in to swim hard and fast to the reef and back.

You'd better find another cure. There'll be no swimming tonight. You're stuck here with the kid.

First thing tomorrow he'd see about arranging Molly to babysit for Rachel. The sooner the better, then he wouldn't go putting his hand up and agreeing to come over here. He should never come near this house again. It was almost as bad as getting up close to the doc herself. It undid all his resolve to steer clear of her. Tantalising as she was. He'd finish the swimming lessons and fade into the background. Out of harm's way.

CHAPTER FOUR

'TERESA, this is Dr Rachel. She's going to help us get your baby out.' Manea had such a relaxed air about her that her patient didn't seem to understand she might be in trouble.

'Hello, Teresa. I'll examine you once Manea's given me some details.' Rachel slipped on gloves as she listened to the midwife.

'Blood pressure's peaked and the contractions are under four minutes apart,' Manea told her. 'This is Teresa's second pregnancy, and she's at thirty-nine weeks.'

Rachel asked Teresa, 'Did you have any problems with your first baby?'

'She popped out early. I didn't even make it to the hospital.' Teresa's grin quickly changed to a grimace as a contraction gripped her. 'Think I liked it better when the baby came fast.'

Rachel smiled. 'I can understand that.'

'You've got one boy, haven't you, Doc?' Teresa asked. 'I've seen him playing next door at Lissie's house. You've got to watch he doesn't get that white skin sunburned.'

Rachel again smiled. 'I bought a bucketful of sunscreen the day we arrived.' After the examination Rachel straightened. 'Okay, Teresa, your baby is trying to come out bottom first.' She squeezed her patient's hand. 'Don't worry, though. We're here to help. Have you got a partner here with you?'

Teresa told her, 'He's waiting at home. He'll come when baby's been born.'

Manea asked quietly, 'You're not doing a C-section?'

'Too late for that.'

The midwife sighed. 'I guess I just thought you would. I'm not used to working with a specialist any more.'

'A Caesarean might've been an option if Teresa had presented a few hours earlier. Anyway, natural birthing will have less impact on her in the long run.' Rachel crossed to the basin and began rewashing her hands.

In a few minutes everything was ready. Now it was up to the baby. 'When you have the next contraction, can you push hard, Teresa?' Then moments later, 'That's it. One side of baby's bottom is coming. Another big push. Yes, that's great. Here we go. And another. Now we've got both sides out. There are the legs.' Finally Rachel had the infant's mouth and nose clear of the birthing passage and she breathed a sigh of relief. 'Nearly there.' Suddenly her hands were filled with the warm, slippery body of a brand-new life.

Rachel's heart leapt in her throat as she gazed down at the scrunched-up little face. Wow. She never ceased to be amazed at the first sight of a newborn. It was a wondrous moment, made all the more poignant ever since she'd had Riley.

Manea lifted the boy into a warm blanket and wiped out the tiny mouth, before using suction to clear his airways. 'Here you are, Teresa. Meet your son.'

Teresa stared at her boy, fat tears rolling down

her cheeks. 'He's beautiful,' she whispered. 'Manea, can you ring Taunga for me? He'll be so excited he's got a boy this time.'

Hot tears slid from the corners of Rachel's eyes too as she watched the young mother bonding with her second child. *Will I ever have another baby? A brother or sister for Riley? Guess I have to have a man in my life for that to happen. Not just any casual man either, but a loving, caring one who is prepared to stay around for ever.*

Why did the name Ben Armstrong spring to mind?

Rachel turned into Ben's drive and parked his car. She felt wired. Helping deliver a baby often did that. Watching the joy break out on Teresa's face, and then a little while later on Taunga's, had been very special.

Moments like these always brought back memories of the first time she'd held Riley in her arms, his first angry cry, the reverence in Jamie's eyes as he'd taken Riley from her and stared into his son's face.

Jamie. Some time she was going to have to let him go. But it was hard. She missed him. And Riley needed him, big time. For all those things that only a dad could show his son.

The things that Ben had started to show him.

The thought stabbed her heart. Ben. Big, strong, good-looking Ben. On the outside very similar to Jamie. Was that the attraction for her? Was she substituting one man for the other? No, definitely not. Anyway, Jamie had had problems, starting with a belief that he was invulnerable in dangerous situations that sensible people knew to avoid. Or at least go into cautiously.

Ben always stepped up to help people. Did he ever take it that bit further so that he was endangering himself?

The answers weren't forthcoming. She knew little about her neighbour despite the heat that zapped between them. And sitting here in his car wasn't changing a thing. She shoved the door open, clambered out. The air was cooler tonight, thank goodness. She might get to sleep right through—when she finally felt calm enough to go to bed. Babies. Ben. Both romped around her skull as she ducked through the fence and headed to her house.

'I hear Teresa had a healthy boy. She loves her new doctor too.' Ben sat on her deck, his legs stretched out in front of him, his back against the wall.

One day she'd get used to how quickly word got around this place. 'Everyone's happy and healthy. Mission accomplished.' She sank onto the top step. 'You could've gone inside, you know.'

'Prefer it out here.'

'How's Riley? Did he wake?'

'Not a peep.'

'All that swimming exhausts him, in a good kind of way.' It exhausted her too, being a totally unfit person who thought any form of exercise was for the birds. She glanced up at Ben. Faint light from the hall accentuated his strong jawline, his wide shoulders. 'Thank you for teaching him. It's great for his confidence.'

'Like he lacked confidence.'

She grinned. 'You're right.' Then her grin slipped.

'It took a knock when Jamie died, but it seems he's getting it back now. I just hope it's not temporary, all tied into the newness of his strange home and latest friends.'

'He'll have other bad days.' Ben spoke with knowledge in his tone. 'Moving on doesn't happen in one hit. It's more like a see-saw, springing up, dropping down. But the upward times eventually get bigger, stronger.'

Is that how it was for Ben when his wife had died? 'You're right. I just worry about the long-term effect on him of losing a parent so young.'

'Kids are more resilient than adults.'

'You think?'

He didn't answer and an easy silence fell between them. Rachel listened to the night. There was very little movement on the road now, the endless stream of scooters having finally stopped. The restaurants were in darkness. The tourists were probably in their hotels or rental homes. Being early risers, the locals would be in bed. The only clear sound was the soft swish of the sea beyond as it unfurled on the sand.

She smiled. Already she'd come to love that sound. It helped her relax, sometimes even sent her to sleep at night. It was a constant that helped her settle into her new home so far from people she loved. There hadn't been time to miss anyone yet, and hopefully when she did she'd be so ensconced here that she'd brush that homesickness off.

'How do you cope with your loss?' Ben's deep voice broke into the magic.

Shocked that someone as reticent as Ben would even ask, she snapped, 'Day by day.' Some days she didn't think she'd ever recover. Uncomfortable now, she stood up. 'I'm going to make a cup of tea. Want one?'

'Sure.'

Did nothing perturb him? She was angry with him and he just carried on sitting on the deck. She'd offered tea out of politeness, hoping he'd actually take his leave. But no. It was after midnight and he was hanging around as if he had no place to go. 'How do you have it?'

'Black and strong.'

'No sugar?'

'You think I need sweetening up?'

No, he was sweet enough really, underneath that bear-like exterior. 'Three spoonfuls?'

'Sorry, Doc. I know how it is when people ask you how you're doing. Most of them don't have the tiniest clue what it's like.'

'But you do.' And she instantly forgave him. 'It's worse when friends and family say you should be pulling yourself together by now.'

'That's why I left New Zealand.'

'When Jamie first died I went through all the usual emotions, I guess.' She leaned against the railing, thinking back to those dreadful days when her mind had been numb with grief. 'Then I got angry.'

'Apparently that's normal too.'

'No, really angry because Jamie didn't have to die that day. It was his fault.' She nibbled at a fingernail. 'Sometimes I think the rage takes over. I might've let it rule my choices about the future. If I'd stepped away from it maybe I could've got my life back on track and not left London.'

'You think coming here was a mistake?'

All the way out from England she'd wondered if it was. Had she let Lissie talk her into something because it had become too tiring to keep on fighting her friend's gentle but relentless persuasion? And now? Now she conceded Lissie might've been right. This place could heal her. Perhaps it had already begun.

Rachel turned to face Ben. 'It's too soon to know.' If only it was light enough to read the expression in those dark eyes. 'But I think I might have done something right for the first time in ages. Right for Riley, right for me.'

'Might even be right for me,' Ben murmured aloud thirty minutes later as he slid under the sheet and spread out over his bed, his hands behind his head. Wide awake, his mind kept replaying that conversation with the doc about getting her life sorted.

'She's so vulnerable.'

Hell, he was vulnerable. He still hadn't put Catrina's death behind him. Hadn't even started to.

That's because you deliberately hold onto the grief and despair to avoid considering you might actually be a tiny bit happier these days now that you've given up the medical career that was strangling you.

Where had that come from? Ben sat up, stared around the dark room looking for something, someone, to yell at. Strangling him? Giving him nightmares, more like. Years ago, when he'd been a child, one of his father's shepherds had had a quad bike roll over on him. The bike had been too heavy for the eleven-year-old Ben to shift, and the man's agonised screams had sent him racing over the hills for home and help. The incident had made him a hero in everyone's eyes—except his. That had been when the idea of becoming a doctor had begun to grow. He'd believed then he'd be able to help people, do something for their pain. He'd got that damned wrong, hadn't he?

One thing he'd learned about himself throughout his medical training had been that his inability to endure watching other people suffer had nothing to do with how he could help alleviate their anguish. He could pump patients full of morphine, set their broken bones, diagnose their conditions, but he'd never been able to get past their pain. Their eyes would beseech him to take away the agony gripping them. Agony that widened their eyes, or squeezed them tight. Agony that left their lips taut and white. Made their hands into fists, strained their muscles to breaking point. And he hadn't been able to bear that. Even when the drugs he'd administer had begun to work, he'd hated to watch the patient.

He hadn't understood where the deep-seated sense of helplessness, of inadequacy had come from, but it had made him question what he was doing, being a doctor. Catrina's accident had been the final straw. Having to watch the woman he loved with all his heart suffer untold agony had devastated him. He'd struggled not to look away through her last minutes. When the paramedics had arrived and given her morphine, which had dulled those beautiful eyes, his relief had been out of proportion to the grief that had already gripped him. That's when he'd given up his medical career.

What would Catrina say if she could see you now?

Ben jerked upright again. Damn it, he didn't need this. He'd go for a run. In the dark? Yeah. He didn't make a move towards getting off the bed, though.

Instead he enunciated loudly the words that had been stuck in his craw for too long. 'Catrina would be disappointed with me.'

She'd known he'd been considering giving up medicine for quite a while, and she hadn't been happy. In her opinion, he should think about the whole picture and how he saved people, not about what they had to endure before they got better.

Damn it. This was stuff he didn't think about, ever. Yet now, over the space of a few days, one woman had begun turning his head, making him face up to the things he'd done a superb job of avoiding for years. He missed his old life. A lot. He missed Catrina big time. But slowly, slowly, she was leaving him, easing out of his psyche.

And as she did so, a big hole was opening up that he wanted to fill with other opportunities. Other people.

Like Rachel. Like her son. Like the possibility of children of his own.

His pillow hit the far wall. His feet slammed onto the wooden floor. His T-shirt tugged on his ear as he shoved into it. The laces of his running shoes slithered through his fingers as he tried to tie them up.

The road wasn't long enough as he pounded down it.

He did not need Rachel in his life. He did not need anyone. Catrina had been his one true love. And he'd completely screwed that up. From that day on he'd set about creating a life where he let no one in. A goddamned lonely life.

'Catrina? Can you hear me?' He glared up at the sky as he ran, despair pouring from him along with his sweat. 'I need you, babe. Tell me what to do. Tell me how to let you go and yet still keep hold of you.'

He tripped over something solid in the middle

of the road. His arms windmilled through the air in his futile attempt to remain upright. The tarmac was hard when his knees and forearm slammed down onto it, the rough surface sand-papering his skin.

A dog shunted up onto its feet and strolled off the road. The air turned blue with expletives as Ben dragged himself upright and turned for home, hobbling awkwardly.

If that had been a message from Catrina then he was in big trouble.

Rachel waved to Ben as she began reversing down the drive on the way to work the following morning. Then she braked, wound down her window. 'Are you all right?'

Ben limped towards his police truck. 'Yep.'

Then she noticed the raw flesh on his arm. 'What happened to your arm?'

'Tripped over a ruddy dog.' He slipped into the vehicle and slammed the door shut, leaned out the window. 'Riley, coming swimming tonight, mate?'

Mate. These two were on good terms. Meanwhile, Rachel seemed to be being pushed aside, told to mind her own business in a slightly less than direct way.

'Yes,' Riley yelled as though Ben was on the other side of the island. 'Can't wait.'

'See you then.' Ben waved to Riley, not her, and roared out onto the road.

Rachel stared after the departing truck. Sometimes that man was too rude for his own good. She'd been friendly, asking after an obvious injury. Next time she'd ignore him, even if he arrived on crutches and wrapped in bandages.

Thankfully her morning improved, along with her temper, after dropping Riley off at Lanette's. At work patients and staff seemed more than happy to talk to her endlessly about family and friends and their illnesses.

A little before midday Manea picked up the last patient file from Rachel's desk and headed for the door. 'That's me done for the day, unless my sister's baby makes an appearance.'

'I thought she had a week to go.' Rachel scratched through her memory to the file on Manea's sister.

'Her three other babies arrived early so we're expecting the same this time. Which would be good because I've got a wedding to go to on the proper due date.' Manea laughed. 'She'll probably be on time as a way of paying me back for all the mean tricks I played on her when we were little.'

The phone on Rachel's desk rang, putting an end to their chatter. 'Dr Simmonds speaking.'

'Doctor, this is Sam Carter from the medical centre. I'm sorry I missed you when you visited last week. I'd hoped to catch up with you before now. Unfortunately I've got an urgent case for you.'

'What's the problem?'

'A twenty-five-year-old tourist has come in with acute abdominal pain and nausea, some shoulder pain. She says she's eight weeks overdue with her menstrual cycle and I'm suspecting an ectopic pregnancy,' Sam told her.

Wonderful. No means of doing an ultrasound to

be absolutely sure of a diagnosis. Rachel's head began to pound. Here was the reality of working in a remote land. 'Send her straight over. I'll be waiting.'

'Her name's Jennifer Tipping, and, Rachel...' Sam paused. 'She's getting married tomorrow, so as you can imagine she's absolutely distraught.'

'The poor girl.' Rachel's heart squeezed in commiseration. 'It could be a bedside service if the hospital management are happy with it.' Certainly nothing like the beach setting the woman had probably been looking forward to for months.

'She says she'll postpone if she has to have surgery.'

'I'll keep you posted.'

When Jennifer and her fiancé arrived they both looked stricken. 'We've been so excited about the wedding. All our friends and family paid a heap to come over for it and now it's not going to happen,' the woman wailed.

'Let me examine you first before you start cancelling everything.' Rachel slipped on latex gloves and helped Jennifer onto the bed while her partner stood staring out the window. 'If I do have to operate, you might be well enough in two days for the ceremony. You won't be having races up and down the beach by then, but I don't suppose they were part of the wedding plans, anyway.'

'Doctor, just do something about the pain.' Jennifer winced as Rachel's fingers probed her abdominal wall.

'How long have you been feeling unwell?'

Jennifer shook her head. 'I'm not sure. Quite a while, I think, but I put it down to all the running around getting ready for the wedding. Today's different. I feel really sick and my shoulder is giving me grief.'

Rachel began an internal examination. 'Did you know you were pregnant?'

'No.' Jennifer groaned. 'We got a big surprise when the GP did a urine test for me, didn't we, Harvey?'

Harvey answered without turning around. 'Sure did. Don't know how that happened.' The guy's neck reddened. 'Well, I mean…' He spluttered to a stop and stared at something outside.

Rachel smoothed over the poor guy's discomfort. 'Babies have a habit of making their own minds up about things right from the get-go.' Then she added quietly, 'But this one appears to have gone the wrong way and is growing in your Fallopian tube. I'm going to have to do a laparoscopy to remove the embryo. This means I might be able to save your tube, and there'll only be a tiny scar by your tummy button.'

Jennifer paled. 'Will I be able to have children in the future? We definitely want a family. Don't we, Harvey?'

Now Harvey did look around. He crossed to place an arm around Jennifer's shoulders. 'Of course we do.'

'If I can save the tube then you'll be fine. And even if I can't, you've still got a second tube, and plenty of women go on to have healthy pregnancies in the same situation.' Rachel lifted the phone to call the theatre nurse.

Jennifer asked, 'Are you sure this isn't appendicitis?'

Replacing the phone without dialling, Rachel told the couple, 'It's definitely not. The pain is very similar but that shoulder pain indicates internal bleeding, which you don't get with appendicitis. I'm sorry, Jennifer.'

'That's okay. You know what you're doing. It's just— The wedding and everything. This was supposed to be the best time of my life and now look at it.' She burst into tears and turned in against Harvey's chest. 'I'm sorry.'

'Hey, stop that. It's not your fault.' The young man dropped a series of light kisses on his fiancée's face.

'I'll be back in a couple of minutes.' Rachel slipped out the door and headed down to Theatre. Those two needed a few minutes by themselves.

CHAPTER FIVE

EFFIE's husband, Hepi, tooted as he backed onto the road after an early barbeque dinner. Effie, Nina and Rosy all hung out the windows, yelling goodbye.

Rachel grinned as she waved back. 'Another day in Paradise nearly over.'

She headed inside to her spotless kitchen. Effie had refused to leave until she and the girls had cleaned up.

'What's Paradise?' Riley asked.

She ruffled Riley's hair. Within weeks he was becoming quite the independent little man about the place, copying Ben's cocky walk, putting his hands on his hips when he wanted to make a point. 'Paradise is a beautiful place where everything is lovely and sunny and friendly.'

Back in London she'd not known what it was

like to be warm—downright roasting at times—
every day. To think she'd brought a load of jer-
seys and jeans with her. They'd probably never be
worn again and there was no point giving them
to a second-hand clothing shop. No one around
here had any use for such heavy clothing.

She loved her daily swim, wearing light tops
and short skirts to work, being able to sit on her
deck in the evenings, listening to the night close
in as the drums beat steadily at the Island Cultural
Show further down the road.

'I'm going to sit outside and listen to the beetles.'
Riley headed for the door. That was another
change. In England Riley would never have
stepped outside in the dark, especially if there
were insects around.

'It's almost bedtime, sweetheart.'

'Tomorrow's Saturday. I can sleep in.'

Rachel shook her head at him. 'Okay, half an
hour extra. But only as a treat.' The roosters that
still woke her at a ridiculously early hour never
bothered him.

Riley raced into the kitchen five minutes later,

his little face contorted with worry. 'Mummy, I can't find Daddy.'

What? For a moment Rachel's mind went blank as she struggled to work out what he meant. How could he find his father? Jamie was buried in England.

'Daddy's star's not up there. Has it crashed out of the sky?'

Relief surged through her. The star they'd selected one night in London that was easy for Riley to find. She was surprised this discussion hadn't happened weeks ago. 'Let's go outside and take a look.'

Riley slid his hand into hers and skipped beside her. 'I need to find Daddy. I want to tell him about the fish Hepi brought for our dinner.'

They sat on the top step and tilted their heads back. 'You know something, Riley? Since we've moved countries we should probably get Daddy to move to a new star. He needs to be in the same part of the world as you.'

Riley's head pressed against her shoulder as he

studied the dark universe with its glittering jewels. 'How would he know to move?'

'You pick a star first. Which one do you think you'll be able to find every night? It should be bigger and brighter than all the others.'

She held her breath while Riley stared upward. If he couldn't decide on a star then there'd be tears, and she hated seeing her little boy getting upset. He'd begun moving on from his terrible loss.

As she had. The thought clanged in her head. She didn't wake every morning wondering how she'd get through the day any more. Her days had purpose now. Her life had purpose. There were lots of women here she could help.

'That one,' Riley cried suddenly. 'See it, Mummy?'

Rachel followed the pointing finger and couldn't decide which of the millions of stars Riley had chosen, but as long as he was happy, what did it matter? 'Okay, now you have to sit quietly and talk to Daddy in your head. Tell him why you've found him a new star and then ask him to cross to it.'

Riley shifted, lying across her thighs, staring up at the sky. His eyes were as big as tennis balls and his lips moved as he talked silently to his father. After a few minutes he blinked and said, 'I've told Daddy what he has to do. I'm going to talk to him again tomorrow night.' A yawn ripped his mouth wide. 'I'm tired now, Mummy. Think I'll go to bed.'

Without being told? Without grizzling and demanding a story? Rachel grinned. The air was definitely different out here. 'Right, let's get you sorted.'

Ten minutes later Riley was sound asleep and Rachel headed for her deck, a glass of lemonade in her hand. She might do some stargazing herself.

Stepping through the front door, she gasped. Lemonade sloshed over her hand. A man leaned against one of the uprights holding the roof over the deck.

'Ben, is that you?' Who else had such wide shoulders? Had such a fierce tilt to his chin?

'Didn't mean to frighten you,' he rumbled.

'You didn't really. Can I get you a drink?'

'Have you got a beer?'

Lucky for him she'd bought some that morning for moments like these. Handing him a bottle, she said, 'I didn't hear you come home or I'd have invited you over for dinner with Effie and the family.'

'Had a drink with the guys after work.'

'What brings you over now?' Even to her ears that sounded as though she was annoyed with him. But as she started to explain he took her breath away.

'I heard Riley talking about the stars.'

'Haven't you got television? I know Rarotonga is friendly but listening in on other people's conversations is taking it too far.'

'I was sitting on my step. Your voices carry.'

'I'll remember that in future.' Not that she had major private discussions with any one.

'The star idea is cool.'

High praise indeed. Rachel sat down on a deck chair and sipped her lemonade. 'It works for Riley. It's been hard for him to grasp that his father has gone for good. When I came up with the suggestion that his dad might be keeping an eye on him from above Riley said he would find his dad's star.'

She looked out over the rough lawn, taking in the palms framing the view. Paradise. One day she'd wake up and find herself back in cold London and realise this had all been a dream. *You'd better not. This place is good for you.* 'I only hope I'm not creating a bigger problem and that Riley thinks his father is up there and about to return. Hard to know with someone so young.'

'I reckon he knows exactly what's happened. Like any of us, he's clinging to the hope he's wrong. Give him time. He'll get there.'

Rachel's mouth dropped. 'Thanks for the vote of confidence.' She could do with help like this occasionally. Her own mother hadn't been great at sticking up for her, always siding with her father, who had become more remote every year. When her brother had lost both legs in a work-related accident, her father had hurt terribly. When Jamie had died he'd refused to let her or

Riley close at all, rarely visiting or even phoning. He hadn't been able to cope with seeing people he loved get hurt.

Ben turned to study her thoroughly. 'You do fine as a mum.'

Disconcerted, she sipped her drink again. This was definitely a different Ben from the one she'd become used to.

He swigged his beer and her eyes fixed on his throat, saw him swallow, then he wiped his mouth with the back of his hand, and shocked her further. 'How did Riley's dad die?'

Whoa. Did she want to talk about this? With Ben? Here only Lissie and Pita knew what had happened and she was happy with that. But Ben was becoming important to her. He deserved some sort of answer. 'Like you, he was a cop.' Jamie had been a hero, a goddamned fool of a hero. He'd loved the thrill of danger, the heart-stopping excitement of putting himself out there, testing the odds. Pity he hadn't known when to back off. He'd owed her more respect than that. He'd owed his son. 'He died in a raid on a P lab.'

'Detective?'

'No, those guys spent far too much time sitting on their butts drinking coffee for his liking. His words, not mine. He was an action man, loved taking down his prey.' Thought he was invincible.

'So what went wrong with the raid?' Ben's voice was tight.

Rachel stood up and crossed to stand at the top of the steps, stared out beyond the darkened houses. She couldn't see the sea but she could hear the gentle sighing of the waves. 'It was a set-up. The drugs boss got wind of the investigation. He extracted information from an undercover detective and then set him up as bait. Jamie and another guy were shot dead the instant they entered the warehouse.' Because they were so gung-ho. Had Jamie even thought of her or Riley as he'd slipped inside that building, his gun at the ready?

'That was bad.'

'It was stupid. They were supposed to wait until all the teams were in place. My husband wasn't a very patient man. He knew his colleague was in dire straits and wanted to get him out.'

'I can understand that.'

Of course he could. She shuddered. Leap in first, think about it afterwards. That's what these guys did. Except there'd been no afterwards for Jamie. She'd better remember that whenever she felt the sexual pull towards Ben. Which was most of the time. But one hero a lifetime was more than enough. Her head snapped up and she jerked a thumb over her shoulder. 'I've got a little boy in there who misses his father so much it hurts me deep, deep inside.'

'Does he understand what his father tried to do that day?' Ben's gaze settled on her face.

'You mean does Riley know his father was a hero?' The breath she hauled into her lungs was heavy with despair. 'Unfortunately, yes.'

The shutters dropped over those black eyes watching her. Ben leaned back against the pole, slid his free hand into his jeans pocket while tipping the bottle to his lips. All the while still watching her. 'I see.'

'Do you, Ben? Do you know what it's like to tell your child Daddy's never coming home again? To have to tell him over and over because "never" is too huge a word for a little boy to understand? And all because Jamie was being the goddamned hero that day. As he was on more days than I care to think about. Heroes should remember they've got other responsibilities before flinging themselves into the line of fire. Or they should never get married, never have children.'

Rachel sank down into herself. Where had all that come from? Now Ben would have her pegged as a raving lunatic. But she'd meant every word she'd said. She'd loved Jamie with all her heart, and he'd loved her back as much. But why did he have to risk their happiness all the time until finally his luck had run out? She'd begged him to go easy, to be careful when he was at work, but he'd always given her that wide, cheeky smile of his and hugged her tight as he'd reassured her he knew what he was doing. He'd even asked why she had less confidence in him than the police department did. Having never seen him in action, she'd had no answer that he'd listen to. Apparently loving him and hoping they'd spend the rest of their lives together hadn't counted.

Ben trod lightly down the steps. Going already. If only he wouldn't. At the bottom he turned back to her and touched the backs of her hands gripped around her knees. When she looked up those black eyes were filled with anger and something else indefinable. Pain? Did he understand her impotent rage? Had someone hurt him so badly too?

'Ben?' she whispered.

'You're doing fine, Doc.' He bent close, brushed the softest of kisses over her forehead. 'You're gonna make it.'

And he strode down her path to his fence and swung those long legs over the top, headed around to his front door.

Back to calling her Doc. At least she'd had a conversation with him for once. Her fingers touched the spot where his lips had placed that spun-sugar-light kiss. Ben Armstrong had made a friendly overture towards her. Warmth stole through her chilled heart. As far as kisses went, it had been tame, not the passionate ones she dreamt of having with him. But they were never going to have a relationship other than a shaky friendship. Definitely not one that involved lips on lips, tongue meeting tongue, breasts pressed to chest.

Pushing her fingers to her lips, trying to find his scent, feel his lips, she allowed herself to dream. To imagine what it might be like to hold Ben in her arms. To be made love to by him. Even in his solitude, in those quiet moods and few words, his passion shone through. He oozed it in every cocky step he took, every look he gave, in his rare and brief smile. Was he a generous lover? She couldn't imagine him being selfish. Already she'd seen many instances of his generosity with everyone he came across.

Could she love again? Possibly. Another hero type? Definitely not. She'd never sleep at night, wondering if that was the day he wouldn't come home. She would never have children with a man like Ben. That would be irresponsible on her part.

No, her puzzling neighbour was out of bounds to her.

But she could keep on dreaming, couldn't she?

Ben rounded the front of his house and continued down the path that lead out onto the road, crossing and heading down to the beach. His strides lengthened as he followed the water's edge along the still-warm sand.

Hopefully the gentle lapping of the water would calm his tumultuous mind and put a stop to the thoughts chasing around in his head. He jammed his hands into his pockets and dropped his chin to his chest, but his head still buzzed with crazy notions of hauling the doc into his arms and kissing away that agony filling her bluebell eyes. Hell, he *had* kissed her, but not how he'd wanted to. Where had that fortunate spot of self-control come from? Self-preservation, most likely. But how he'd wanted to claim her with his lips, to taste her, to make her smile and banish that grief she wore.

To make her his.

Ben pulled his shirt over his head, shoved his jeans down his legs and stepped out of them. In his boxers he raced for the water's edge, pushed through the sea until it reached his thighs, then dived in deep. The warm salt water did nothing to stop the stream of images of the doc flowing through his head. He stayed under until his lungs were bursting, until they ached with the need for oxygen.

Back on the surface he gasped in mouthfuls of clean air. Wiping his hands down his sopping hair and face, he lay back and stared up at the stars. And relived the moment he'd leant close to her, smelt her intoxicating fragrance in her hair, felt her warmth. The combination of those things had turned him on something terrible. He had wanted Rachel instantly.

Damn it. He wanted her now. Here. Anywhere. Hard and fast. Her pliant body wrapped around his, taking his length inside her.

He continued to stare up at the sky, willing his rapidly beating heart to slow down, take a break, behave. Nothing was going to happen between him and the doc tonight, or on any other god-damned night. Or day.

Flipping over, Ben swam out towards the reef, long, driving strokes that propelled him through the water. He concentrated on perfection, banishing any other thoughts. But when he heard the waves crashing on the reef he stopped to tread water, breathing rapidly. And immediately thought about the doc.

He should head into town, have a few more beers with the boys, and maybe link up with one of the usual collection of willing female tourists out for a good time. That had always worked in the past, feeding a hunger without having all the day-to-day rubbish to go with it.

But tonight that didn't appeal. Not a jot. Face it, it hadn't appealed since the first moment he'd set eyes on Rachel. One look and all his convictions about never getting involved had vamoosed, no matter how sane and sensible those convictions were. Knowing the agony of loving and losing, knowing how much had been taken from him last time, hadn't been enough to banish from his brain that fascinating, sexy woman back in her cottage next to his. That first night he met her he'd come to the conclusion he'd been too long without a woman. A good bonk was the answer. And had he had one? No. Why not? Because every time he thought about it Rachel slipped into his head, as though she had some claim on him. Which was utterly ridiculous.

Rachel had no place in his life. No one did any more. It might be a lonely life. It might be uninspiring and lacking in real purpose. But it was safe. He couldn't get hurt again. More importantly, he couldn't let down anyone who relied on him for their well-being. He was a cop, all responsibility and no care.

You really believe that? When you stood up to Kepu Vaagana's flying fists last month so you could talk him down from his drug-induced high? When you made sure Effie had speedy treatment? Yes, well, that went with the territory. Had nothing to do with caring about people, with letting them so close he'd have to look out for them all the time, not just through work.

Back on the beach Ben dropped onto the sand and leaned back on his elbows. He loved this place with its easy-going people and total lack of pretension. Leaving Wellington and his medical career had been a brainwave that he'd never regretted for a minute. Becoming a cop at the age of thirty-two had been hilarious, but nothing too strenuous. The biggest crimes were theft and a few fights. Those things were common anywhere in the world, but at least here the police weren't usually dealing with murder, drug manufacturing or extortion.

He'd never have joined the force back home, but coming to the Cook Islands it had made perfect sense to sign up. He liked serving people, and here was a place and job where he could do that without being put in situations where he felt helpless.

Looking up at the star-filled sky again, he thought of the kid. 'Which star did you pick out for your dad? You're a brave wee man. But that's no surprise. You've got a brave mum. A strong, fiercely protective mum who loves you with all her heart.' That love was always there, in her eyes, her facial expressions when talking to the kid, in the way she put him before herself, before a patient.

Was that how she'd loved her husband? Lucky man if she had. She would have. The doc didn't do anything by halves. Lucky, lucky guy. So why had he charged into that warehouse with complete disregard for his own safety?

'Hell, if I had Rachel to come home to at the end of every day I'd be careful crossing the street, let alone going up against armed crims.'

Kerthunk. A coconut fell to the ground. Ben grinned at the sound that was such a part of this place. His grin faded. Falling coconuts also killed a handful of people every year. Did the doc know about the dangers of standing under palm trees? Had she warned the kid to stay away from them?

Note to self: tell the doc first thing tomorrow.

Which meant seeing her. Warmth seeped under his skin. Hang on, wasn't he meant to be staying away from her?

Leaping to his feet, he headed for home. So

much for clearing his head. Now he was more confused than ever. But one thing he did know. There would be no fraternising with Rachel. He'd ask Effie to warn her about the coconuts.

The doc and the kid were better off without him to mess up the life they were getting very comfortable with. They'd both taken to the island lifestyle as though born to it. One day little Riley would want to go out into the big, wide world to get a better education than was available here, but this place would give him stability and support to fall back on when things went pear-shaped. As they invariably would do from time to time. People always returned to the islands and their families when they needed a break from the hassles of the cities down in New Zealand. He could understand why they did that. This place was special. He felt the same. He'd made his home here.

But Rachel's initial contract was for twelve months, though already, according to Lissie, there was talk of making the position permanent. Would Rachel choose to stay on? Long term? Not likely. One day she'd want better opportunities for Riley. Would she send him to boarding school in England or New Zealand? Or would she move away to be with him while he went to day school? Ben sighed. He already knew the answer to that. She was all Riley had, so she'd go with the boy.

What was it to him what Rachel chose to do? He was having no part of her life other than being a good neighbour and maybe sharing an occasional barbeque at the end of a particularly trying day. And from now on he'd make sure there were other people around whenever they did that.

Somehow all this conjecture made him incredibly sad.

Stick to the rules. No dating. No hot sex. No nothing. Rachel was out of bounds. For ever. For her sake.

CHAPTER SIX

'COLLEEN, what on earth are you doing?' Rachel stared at the backside poking out from under her secretary's desk.

'Having a tidy-up' came the muffled reply. Then Colleen wriggled out backwards and squatted on her haunches. 'There's a stack of old newspapers and forgotten files under there.'

She began hauling everything out and Rachel picked up a couple of papers, idly reading the headlines. Mostly political arguments and local news. 'It's a very robust little paper.'

'Take a look at this one.' Colleen passed her the paper she'd been gazing at. 'It's from last year.'

Rachel read the headline: *Local Policeman Is a Hero.* Her stomach squeezed tight.

Senior Constable Ben Armstrong has been heralded as a hero today after he leapt into the stormy sea to rescue two boys who got into difficulties outside the fishing clubrooms. The boys had taken their father's boat without permission. A squall struck the dinghy, overturning and sinking it. Armstrong saw the boys in trouble and swam out to rescue them.

Nausea clawed up Rachel's throat. She slapped the paper down on Colleen's desk. A hero. Another wretched hero. Someone who would put other people's lives before his. Fine, very noble, but what about the people he left behind if, when, something went wrong? So what that there didn't appear to be anyone important in his life at the moment? As if he'd switch off that urge to charge in blindly when there was.

'Rachel? Are you all right?' Colleen's worried voice seemed to come from a long way away.

Rachel blinked, focused on her secretary. 'I'm fine. Truly.' Convincing Colleen or herself? 'I'm going to grab a coffee, then I'll start clinic.'

Colleen picked up a bundle of papers. 'I'll take

these out to the Dumpster. Want me to get that coffee for you on the way back?'

'Okay, thanks. I'll go and introduce myself to the women while you're doing that.' And try to ignore the message pounding in her skull.

Ben's a hero.

She had to stay away from him. She might be enjoying his company but she couldn't allow anything stronger than friendship to develop between them. To fall in love with him would be irresponsible. Her heart would not survive another loss like the last one.

Rachel sank down on her chair, staring blindly out the window. No, she wasn't falling in love again. She'd only known the man four weeks. *It only takes a moment if he's the right person.* No—what she felt for Ben was physical, brought on by a lack of a sex life. Back in England it hadn't occurred to her that she should get out and about, start dating. She hadn't been ready. She still wasn't ready. Despite the longings and needs that swamped her body in the middle of the night sometimes. Sometimes? Try most nights since she'd arrived in Rarotonga.

Since she'd met Ben.

Tears pricked her eyelids. What was she doing, thinking about Ben and love in the same sentence? It could not happen. Neither did she want Riley getting too close, seeing Ben as a father figure. One thing she knew with absolute certainty was that her son would not cope if something happened to Ben too. Already he had a hero-worship thing going on for their neighbour.

There was that word again. Hero.

That article was a timely warning. She'd keep her distance from the man. She'd stop going swimming with him. Unfortunately Riley would be upset. He loved his time in the water with Ben and sometimes his little friends joined them too. Was she being unfair? Probably, but as a responsible parent she was only trying to protect her boy. Overprotective? She had no answer for that.

Movement outside snagged her attention. An elderly man and a young child were making their way slowly across the lawn. The child held the man's arm, gently leading him towards a park bench under a tree. A simple thing but it made Rachel's heart swell with sadness. Riley's grandparents lived half a world away. When would he see them again? Would he grow up respecting his elders if he didn't interact with them?

He'd be fine. There were plenty of older folks here he was meeting, like Lissie's in-laws. But Riley needed a man's guiding hand. She believed she could provide most things he needed, but he was a boy, and boys needed men in their lives. Good men who set good examples.

Okay, so Riley could continue to go swimming with Ben but she'd remain at home. She trusted Ben with her son. There was no need for her to sit on the beach, watching them frolicking in the water, or get in the water with them. They might even have more fun without her there to worry every time Riley took seconds longer to surface from a shallow dive than she thought safe. But she'd have a word to Ben about staying away from showing him any hero tactics.

'Here's your coffee.' Colleen bustled into the room.

Sighing, Rachel took the proffered mug. 'Thanks. Let's get this clinic moving.'

Laughter and loud chatter greeted Rachel as she stepped into the waiting room outside the clinic. Ten pairs of friendly eyes settled on her. 'Hello, ladies.'

'Hello, Doctor,' they all called.

She quickly outlined the smear process. 'If you want one of your friends with you while I examine you, that's okay with me.' From the files she'd read first thing that morning she knew most of these women had never had a smear done. The process often made women nervous and Rachel was all for anything that helped relax her patients.

One of the older women spoke up. 'I'm glad we can do that, Doctor. But our friends won't see anything...' She paused. 'You know, private, will they?'

'Not at all. You'll have a sheet over you.' Rachel sat down amongst the women and sipped her coffee. 'What else can I tell you before we get started?'

At first the women were hesitant but soon the questions were flowing and the laughter grew louder as they teased each other about having a doctor look at their 'front bottoms'.

After ten minutes the woman who'd asked about what her friend might see stood up. 'I'm ready to do this, Doctor. Daphne, you can come and hold my hand and then the doctor can take your slide too and I'll hold your hand.'

Rachel led the way into her room, thinking how wonderful these women were. They epitomised her new home town.

Everything went well until the seventh woman walked into Rachel's office and sat down.

'It's Liu, isn't it?' Rachel asked, and when the woman nodded, she continued, 'You don't need someone with you?'

'No, I'm good to go.'

'Then I need you to take off your skirt and panties and get up on the bed. You can put that sheet over you when you're ready.'

Soon Rachel began an external examination of Liu's abdomen. 'How many babies have you had?' she asked as her probing fingers found an abnormality.

'Four. All girls and they are lots of mischief.'

Rachel didn't mention the small, solid lump as she proceeded to make an internal exam and take a sample for the smear test. 'When did you last have a smear done?'

Liu was the only woman in this morning's group who'd had this done before. 'When my third started school, about five years ago. We lived in Auckland then.'

Too long ago. 'Ideally these should be done every three years. Are your periods regular?'

'Never. They've always been all over the place. Is something wrong?' The laughter that had dominated Liu's eyes began to fade, worry creeping in around the edges.

'Get dressed and then sit with me.' This was the part of her job Rachel found the hardest, and she wasn't sure how much to tell Liu before she had a definite result from the lab on that smear.

Liu studied her, a grave look on her face. 'Okay. I get it. I've been around long enough to know when things aren't right.' She dressed slowly, thoughtfully, then sat down and said, 'Hit me with it, Doc.'

Liu's inadvertent use of Ben's name for her actually settled Rachel, made her understand that these women were no different from women the world over. Their health was important to them, and if she wasn't totally upfront with Liu she'd be doing her a disservice, not to mention insulting her.

'When I felt your abdomen externally I found a small lump. I don't know for sure what it is but I'm concerned enough to flag your smear for the lab staff to take an extra-careful look at your cells. Until we get those results there's nothing we can do, but I'll be nagging them constantly, believe me.' Rachel paused to give her patient time to absorb what she'd heard. 'I would like you to have a scan, which would mean a trip to Auckland.'

'Are you saying it's cancer?' Liu's voice was low, scared.

'It could be, but let's wait until we have those results. The lump is very small, which is good.' Rachel reached for Liu's hand. It was cold and shaky. She squeezed tighter, tried to instil hope and comfort. 'Don't spend the next week worrying yourself sick.' Rachel dragged up a smile.

'It's okay. I wouldn't have your job for all the islands in the world.' Liu pushed herself up off the chair. 'I'm glad I came to you on my own. I don't want those girls out there knowing anything until I know what this lump is. It might scare them away from having their tests.'

Rachel stood and spread her arms, engulfed this amazing lady in a hug. 'If you need to ask me something, want to talk over anything, call me. Or drop in to see me, either here or at home.'

'My girls want to meet Riley. They've heard lots about him from Lissie's boys. They say he sounds like fun.'

How different this scene was to doctoring back home where your patients knew you only as a specialist. Rachel could feel her chest expanding with pride at Liu's comment. 'I think he is.' Then common sense took over. 'He's very new to the freedom he gets here.'

'Makes you worry, eh? Don't. That Ben is great with the kids. He's taught heaps of them to swim better, and to be safe on the roads and under the trees.' Liu gave her a tired smile. 'I hear he's teaching you to swim too. That's the first time he's done that with an adult.'

Rachel tried to roll her eyes in disgust; failed and probably looked like the town idiot. 'That's because you all know how to swim before you turn two years old.'

'You haven't heard what everyone's saying about you, then.'

Despite knowing she didn't need to hear this and that she'd probably regret asking, Rachel asked, 'And what would that be?'

Liu reached for the door handle. Ready to make a quick escape? 'That you and Ben look good together.' Liu breathed deeply. 'It's nice to see Ben happier. He hasn't had a woman for a long time.'

That…Rachel sucked air through her gritted teeth…*I didn't need to know.*

'Sorry I'm late for Riley's lesson. We had an irate tourist who said his wallet had been stolen from his scooter while he was swimming. Then, just as we'd finished placating him by promising a full-scale investigation—' Ben's mouth twisted into a reluctant smile '—the guy's wife raced in, waving the missing wallet. He'd left it on the bed when he'd changed into his swimming trunks.'

Rachel laughed. 'Of course the guy apologised profusely.' Ben was so much more talkative these days. Liu's words floated through her mind. *Ben hasn't had a woman for a long time. It's nice to see him happy.* Her laughter faded. Surely she wasn't the reason for his happiness? They weren't exactly an item. Besides, Ben definitely hadn't had her.

'You got it.' Ben's smile widened. Then he frowned. 'Where's Riley?'

'With Lissie's boys for the night. They're at a birthday party and then Lissie's taking them around to her in-laws' for a barbeque. Riley was keen to go. I think he misses his grandmother.' Not that he'd ever seen much of her. Dad made sure of that.

Ben studied her from under his eyebrows, his gaze sauntering over her skirt and blouse. 'So why aren't you coming swimming?'

Because I need to put some distance between us. 'Thought I'd have a day off, which is why I'm sitting on my step, watching the world go by.' Her very small world, which she was coming to love. 'I'm exhausted. Two babies by lunchtime. And I had my first clinic today.' She'd sent the smears off on the flight to Auckland with a note for urgency on Liu's form. Not that cytology specs were often fast-tracked but with a bit of luck someone would get onto that particular slide more quickly than usual.

'How did that go?'

'They were great, took it all with good grace and a lot of laughter. They're also going to talk their friends into coming to the next clinic.' At least that was the scenario now, but they might change their minds if Liu's results were bad. Rachel was fully aware how people could turn away, go into avoidance mode, rather than look at the situation as a way to save their lives.

'Rachel? Something wrong?'

Ben sat on the step beside her, so close she held herself tight, stiff, in case she inadvertently bumped against him.

She blinked, leaned back against the post as the need to curl in against that broad chest suddenly grabbed her. That would be a mistake so she'd stick to talking.

It'd be wonderful to talk about the clinic and Liu but, of course, she couldn't. She was a doctor; Ben was a policeman. Poles apart when it came to discussing work. Not to mention the confidentiality issue. She did say in an as offhand manner as she could, 'I'm just thinking about one of the patients I examined.'

'Anything wrong?'

'I felt something out of the ordinary. I've done a smear and now have to wait until the results are back.' It was good to share this, even though she couldn't say too much for fear of breaking confidence with Liu.

'Too far along to be mild dysplasia if you felt a lump.'

She blinked. He knew this stuff? 'I'm afraid so.'

'That's hard. Especially on your first clinic. What were the odds of that?' Ben was still studying her in that enigmatic way of his.

'Quite high, I imagine. Take into consideration these women haven't been having regular smears.' Then she added, 'That's the worst-case scenario. But it threw me to get something today when my biggest concern had been making sure the women were comfortable with the process.'

Ben's hand covered her knee. His thumb drew circles on her skin. 'From what people are saying about you around here, you've won everyone over.'

'Really?'

'Really.'

'Wow.'

'Wow.' Ben gave her a long, slow smile that

heated her up more quickly than a blowtorch could have.

Abruptly she leapt to her feet. 'Do you want a cold drink?' *She* needed an icy plunge-pool.

Ben stood up too and gazed down at her. 'Let's go into town for that drink. We can follow it up with a meal.'

'You're asking me out?' On a date? Where was Riley when she needed him? As an excuse? *You don't need one. Go and have some adult time while you've got the opportunity.* Excitement began fizzing through her.

'Yeah.'

'Oh, okay.'

Ben chuckled, low and sexily. 'Should I take that as a yes, then?'

'I'll change into something more appropriate.' A knee-length skirt and a sleeveless shirt that barely touched her midriff was fine for sitting on her deck, but not for a date. A date. With Ben. What was that word? Wow. That's it. Wow.

'No need. This is Rarotonga, capital of casual.'

'Oh, okay.' *Grab your handbag and go have some fun.* 'I'll close up the house.' *Before I come up with a hundred reasons why this could be a mistake.*

Ben leaned in and placed his lips on hers. 'What's the sudden hurry?' he murmured into her mouth. Then before she could think of anything to say his hands took her shoulders to gently bring her closer to his body. His lips pressed harder against hers, and his tongue sought entrance to her mouth.

Rachel swayed into his kiss and embrace, and she kissed him back with all the intensity of the need for this man that had been building up since that night she'd opened her front door to find him standing there. She'd been denying her need for ages, and now she couldn't pretend she didn't want him. Heck, he tasted good. And could he kiss. A kiss that made every nerve ending spark alive, every sensory fibre in her body beg for more. A kiss that hopefully would never end.

Greedily she pushed even closer. All the better to feel as many as possible of his well-developed muscles against her. His chest was hard against her breasts. His arms now tight around her back, holding her to him, holding her upright. Sliding her hands under his shirt, her fingers spread over his skin—feeling, enjoying, teasing that silken texture. Every one of her fingertips sent desire screaming back to her body, demanding more of Ben.

Slowly Ben's mouth left hers, his lips pulling away as though afraid to break contact. He didn't have to stop, damn it. Why had he? Reluctantly she looked up into his eyes, locked heated gazes. Her tongue slid across her bottom lip, and his eyes followed the movement. She stretched up onto her toes, intent on returning to kissing him.

A quick flick of his head and he stepped back one tiny step. 'Time to head into town. Let's not rush things. We've got all night ahead of us.'

All night? As in more kisses? As in making love? Rachel swallowed hard. She could do that. Now that she'd finally shared a kiss with Ben she most definitely did not want to stop at kissing. But he was right. They did have all night so why rush it?

* * *

Ben settled Rachel at a table and went to order two beers. They'd decided to sit outside to make the most of the light evening breeze coming off the sea only metres away.

Rachel luxuriated in the happiness bubbling through her veins. She brushed her swollen lips lightly with her fingertips, reliving every detail of that kiss. Ben certainly knew what he'd been doing. But even better there'd been that startled surprise in his eyes when he'd pulled his mouth from hers. His voice had been rougher than ever when he'd told her it was time to go to town. He'd been as affected by the chemistry between them as she had.

Glancing across to the bar, she watched him lean nonchalantly on the counter and talk to the barman. All casual calm, as if nothing had happened between them, as if he hadn't mentioned anything about the rest of the night.

He turned, caught her staring at him and winked.

Rachel grinned and straightened her back. Two could play that game.

As he strolled back to her, two beers wedged between the fingers of one hand, women stopped talking to watch his progress, admiring his physique. A lick of pride that it was her he'd chosen to be with added to her sense of well-being, boosting her self-confidence.

Tonight she'd have some fun. She hadn't had time away from Riley, except to go to work, since—since she'd become a widow. Her shoulders tightened. Tonight she'd begin living again, here, in a country that had already wound its magic around her, with a man who seemed to be doing the same. For once she'd ignore all the warning lights going off in her head. They'd have a few drinks, enjoy a meal, repeat that heartstopping kiss, and maybe get down and dirty together. She already knew Ben would be a fantastic lover. His kiss had been generous and exciting.

'What's that smug smile about?' Ben slid a bottle across the table to her.

Not even the cool offshore breeze could prevent the heat scorching her cheeks. 'Nothing.' She gulped at the beer and choked.

Instantly Ben was behind her, tapping her firmly between the shoulder blades with his open palm. 'Steady.'

She gasped, coughed, wiped the back of her hand over her mouth. 'I'm fine, thanks.' A little wired, but fine.

The table rocked as Ben settled onto the seat next to her—as in bodies-touching-all-down-one-side next to her. Her heart knocked her ribs as if to say, Hello, here we go. A night to remember. This time when she lifted her bottle to her lips with a hand that wasn't quite steady, her sip was cautious. As much as she liked Ben's hand on her back, being lightly thumped wasn't what she had in mind.

'Is this a regular haunt of yours?' she asked.

'One of them.'

'A man about town, are you?' She grinned at him.

'That's me.' He smiled back.

Instantly her muscles turned to putty as thoughts

of kissing those lips returned. Which was a bad idea if she wanted to enjoy the whole night, not just a small part of it. Fishing around for something to keep her mind on more mundane matters, she asked, 'You come here with your workmates? Or other friends?' She really didn't know much about him.

'Both.'

'Are you into any sports? Play rugby or soccer?'

'Golf.' He tapped the table with one finger. 'Too hot to be playing rugby. That's for young guys or fools.'

'And you are neither.'

'Thanks. I think.' He traced the wet circle his bottle had made on the table. 'You still happy with your decision to move away from London?'

Whipping her head around, she stared at him. 'I love it here.'

'Just checking. I'm kind of getting used to you being around. If you were thinking of moving on, I'd like some warning, that's all.'

He'd surprised her. He wanted warning if she

was leaving? 'It is bizarre living in a country with a population that would fit into an underground railway station where I come from. Going to work in sleeveless tops and with bare legs is way different to every outfit I've ever worn.'

His face started getting an uncertain look.

Placing a hand over his tapping forefinger, she said, 'Why would I want to leave all that?' She spread her other hand towards the sea. 'This is what dreams are made of. And I get to live it every day. I don't need trains and buses, apartments with no front lawn, hospitals the size of a small city and supermarkets where no one knows me.'

Ben's hand turned under hers, clasped her fingers in a warm hold. 'Good answer.' Then he muttered, 'But it's early days yet.'

She chose to ignore that. Why spoil a wonderful evening arguing about something neither of them had an answer for? Only time would tell if she was going to stay in the islands long term.

They watched the gulls circling overhead, looking for an unsuspecting patron of the bar to leave a plate of food unguarded. On a ramp next door the rowing-club members were landing skiffs and stripping off wetsuits. A smile unfurled deep inside Rachel. 'Yeah, this is pretty damned good. If my former colleagues could see me now, they'd think they'd woken up in the wrong movie.'

A waitress sashayed up to them. 'Another round of drinks?'

'Yes, please,' Ben answered without consulting her.

Rachel's smile widened. Nice to be with someone and have them taking charge for a while. She made so many decisions about her patients, about Riley, that occasionally she appreciated having someone take over.

'What brought you to Rarotonga?' she ventured.

At first she thought he wouldn't answer. His Adam's apple bobbed as he drained his first bottle and set it aside. His gaze scanned the horizon, returned to her. 'After Catrina died I couldn't think straight. Everyone had some advice to offer about what I should be doing. You'd think if they all had my needs at heart they'd have come up with the same or similar suggestions.'

'But they were diametrically opposed?'

'Yeah. From finding work on some alien planet to getting back out there dating everything in a skirt—that's my mates talking—I had more suggestions on fixing my life than you get in one of those self-help books.'

'Unless you've experienced that grief, you don't really understand. People want to help so much but haven't a clue what to do so they drag up any old idea. That makes them feel good.'

Ben's finger stroked the back of her hand. 'I think some of them were relieved when I announced I was joining the police force and moving to the Cook Islands. I solved the problem of me for them.'

'So you haven't always been a cop?' She was sure he hadn't.

'No.' He pulled his hand away.

Oka-ay, that was a no-go zone. 'Tell me about your family.'

Lifting his bottle to his lips, Ben drank deeply.

Silence stretched between them. Had she gone too far with her questions? She'd hate it if she'd spoiled their evening because she wanted to know more about him.

But then he began talking. 'Mum's a hard-working lady who's always cooking meals and looking after an endless stream of old folk at the retirement village where she works. Dad died a few years ago from cancer.' Ben looked out at the water again. The sun had dropped behind the hills, allowing a warm, soft darkness to settle over the island. 'Then there are the brats. My bossy sister and one cheeky brother who is actively avoiding domestic bliss by playing the field hard. And a bundle of cousins who all but grew up on the farm with us.' Love laced his words.

'You must miss them.'

'Miss them? If only I got a chance to. Being the brother and cousin with a house in the islands makes me very popular. Destination Ben's house for all holidays. It's a rare month that I don't have some of them—' he wriggled his forefingers in the air '—dropping in.'

'No one's been since I arrived.'

'They came en masse in early April for my sister's wedding so they're taking a break on holidays. I think the wedding ate up most of their savings.'

'Did they all stay with you?'

'Hell, no. Around at Muri Beach there are plenty of houses rented out to tourists. I found two large ones next door to each other for the tribe. It worked perfectly and Tania was married on the beach with the reception at one of the restaurants that overlooks the lagoon.'

'Sounds wonderful.' Rachel sighed. Rarotonga and weddings went hand in hand. She couldn't think of anywhere more beautiful and romantic for a marriage celebration. Whoops. Where was she going with that thought? Nowhere. She hadn't got back into a single woman's life properly yet. Marriage, if she ever considered it again, was a long way off.

'Hungry?' asked Ben.

'Yes, actually, I am.'

'Okay eating here? We can stay outside and

order pizzas, or go upstairs to the restaurant and see what's on the menu.'

'Out here's perfect.' She couldn't bear to be inside with all the diners she'd seen arriving over the past hour. It would be hot and stuffy, and not so…personal. Sharing pizza with Ben appealed more than anything right now.

CHAPTER SEVEN

AT EIGHT o'clock a band consisting of young lads from the local school started playing and Ben stood, reached down and tugged Rachel to her feet. 'Come on. Let's shake hips.'

'That would have to be the most charming invitation I've ever had.' She smiled that sweet yet sexy and alluring smile of hers.

Gawd help him, but he was a basket case around this woman. She only had to smile and he was blithering. Probably had drool running out of the corner of his mouth. Without thinking, he wiped the back of his hand over his lips. Dry. He grinned. Just went to show how all semblance of sanity disappeared when Rachel appeared. And now they were about to dance together. Already his heart rate had picked up the pace and they hadn't left the table yet.

She took his hand in her soft one and pulled him towards the small square of vacant floor where she turned to face him and began to gyrate those superb hips in time to the beat the boys were pounding out with more enthusiasm than talent. Ben shook his head in amusement. 'How the hell do you do that?'

'Do what?' She didn't stop moving, now holding her arms out and shaking her body at him.

'Dance to that uneven beat.' Could hearts leap out of chests? His felt as though it was about to.

'Easy. Give it a go. Let loose and shake.' Rachel grinned as she showed him exactly what she meant.

She's a goddamned tease. 'I know how to dance, woman.' His feet were glued to the floor.

'Then move those hips.'

Hell, was she seducing him? Or just one of those women who loved to dance to any music whatsoever? Pubs back home were full of them shaking their butts, waving their arms, tossing their long hair. Like the woman in front of him.

He grinned, long and slow, and moved his hips, his feet, finally his whole blasted body.

And Rachel smiled again. Long and slow and sexy. Like a reward. How could he earn another? Except if she kept smiling he'd have to leave the floor. Minutes into the first dance and he was already in trouble. His body was reacting to every move she made and the strain of trying to ignore the need coursing through him was ripping him apart. He should drag her off the floor and take her home, back to her neat little cottage, and push her inside, slam the door and leap the fence back into safety. Safe from smiles that reminded him of all the wonderful sensations brought on by being with a beautiful woman. Safe from the way the scent of lavender on her skin smelt sweeter, riper than he'd ever known it. Safe from losing his heart again.

Ben reached for her hand, raised it above her head and spun her under his arm, tipped her back against him, paused, then spun her back to face him. Damn, that felt good. *He* felt alive, excited.

They spun, jived, shook, drank cold beers, and finally fell into each other's arms and held on.

'I'm whacked,' Rachel muttered somewhere against his chest.

Not too much, I hope. 'Let's grab a taxi and go home.' No way was Ben driving tonight. He'd probably sweated out ninety-nine per cent of the beer he'd drunk but he was a responsible cop.

'Home?' Rachel tensed, leaned back in his arms and tilted her head back so her gaze met his. Her hair had fallen out of the knot she'd somehow tied it into and as she moved it slid tantalisingly slowly across his arms, teasing, promising, cranking tighter the already extreme tension in every muscle of his body.

He leaned over her and kissed those full lips. 'Home.'

In the taxi he placed an arm over her shoulders and tucked her in close to him, but within moments he couldn't do that without wanting to devour her. He kissed her until the taxi driver rapped the window and said, 'We're here, boss.'

Ben tossed the guy a couple of notes, more than

the fare by a lot, and lifted Rachel out onto the roadside. Then he swung her up into his arms and strode purposefully to his front door, which he opened with a well-aimed boot. He didn't bother with lights. Enough moonlight filtered through the windows to show the way to his bedroom where he laid her on his bed.

Rachel instantly sat up and began unhooking the buttons of her blouse. Her eyes were filled with a seductive hunger that turned him on more than any touching or kissing could've done. She wanted him. Badly. That stroked his ego. His boots hit the floor, followed by his jeans and shirt.

Rachel's blouse slid down her arms, pooled at her waist as she reached behind to unhook her bra.

His breath deserted him at the sight of her beautiful breasts. Perfect. He cupped them, his thumbs flicking across her already erect, tight nipples. Her moan was full of ecstasy. Her hips lifted and she shoved that figure-hugging skirt down past her knees, slid her feet out and flipped onto her back.

Ben drank in the sight of her stunning body, his hands tracing a path that followed his greedy gaze from her nipples to the stud in her belly button to the mound hidden by that feminine triangle. 'You're stunning, Rachel. So beautiful.' He followed her down onto the mattress, his mouth tasting her, his tongue slick on her hot skin.

When her hands reached for him, closing around his manhood, sliding down him slowly, firmly, he knew such a raw need he'd never known before. Damn it, everything would be over before he started if she kept stroking him like that.

Dragging his mouth from her skin, he roared, 'Rachel, for pity's sake, slow down so I can give you a good time.'

He felt her hand tighten, move faster. He heard a deep, sexy chuckle. 'You already are, Ben. I do not want to wait. For anything. I've waited weeks. Take me, Ben. Hard and fast. Now.'

How could a bloke deny a lady her wish?

* * *

Rachel stretched, reaching for the bottom of the bed with her toes, and touching the headboard with her hands. Ohh, she felt good, wonderful.

'Stop looking so pleased with yourself.' A deep growl rumbled into the pillow beside her.

'Only showing it how it is.' She dropped her arms and wriggled closer to the source of her contentment.

Ben lifted himself over her, his long body covering hers as he took his weight on his elbows. 'Insatiable, are you?' There was a mischievous glint in his eyes, a hint of pleasure to come.

'Depends what's on offer,' she teased.

'Long.' He nipped her shoulder lightly. 'Slow.' His teeth pinched her bottom lip. 'Very long, very slow.' Those teeth made another sense-firing nip.

Long and slow sounded wonderful. If she could last the distance. 'I'm out of practice.' But thankfully her body knew the moves. She responded passionately to those teeth now grazing over her collarbone and down towards her breasts.

'Looking forward to the day you're up to full

speed,' Ben growled against her breast, before taking a nipple between his lips and sucking hard.

A hot needle of desire pierced her, followed by another and another. 'This is slow?'

'Absolutely.' Ben's hand slid down her side, over her hip and between her legs.

When he shifted off her she tried to beg him not to move. Words failed her. She loved having his body crushing down on hers. She loved feeling the tightening of every one of his muscles, his erection pressing against her. But then his tongue worked a special magic at her centre and she couldn't give a damn where his body had got to—as long as he didn't stop the slow and long strokes building the exquisite tension within her, making her crave release.

'Now,' she cried out.

Ben slowed his pace, but did not stop. He held off giving her the climax she craved. Instead he let her tension ease off and began building it all over again. And again, until she was begging him to join her.

Finally, when she knew she absolutely couldn't

wait another moment, couldn't take another stroke, Ben lifted himself over her and entered her quivering body, and at last gave her what she wanted. Only her climax was way more than she'd ever have believed possible. It took everything away from her except the kaleidoscope of sensations saturating her with mind-numbing feelings of utter wonder. Her hands gripped together behind his back and she held on tight as she fell off the edge of the world.

CHAPTER EIGHT

RACHEL awoke to the sound of her cellphone chirping. When she rolled over to find her hand-bag, which she'd dropped in her haste to make love with Ben last night, she came face-to-face with the man himself. His eyes were open and twinkling at her. His mouth lifted into a smile. 'Good morning, Doc.'

She hesitated. Back to 'Doc' so soon? When she was still in his bed with his hip tucked snugly against hers? 'Morning, Ben,' she said cautiously.

His arm swung up, her handbag swinging from his fingers. 'Looking for this?'

'I guess.' As she scrabbled through the junk in-side the bag she asked, 'What time is it?'

'Sex o'clock.'

Jerking her head up, she clashed looks with him. So the doc thing wasn't bad. 'Who's insatiable now?' She lifted the sheet and peered down the length of his body. 'Definitely you.'

He smiled. Long and slow, of course. His eyes were smoky with desire.

Her heart thumped heavily against her ribs. She was ruined. By this man. If the night they'd shared was a warm-up then she was lost for ever. No other man would ever be able to give her the pleasure Ben had.

Her cell stopped its annoying chirping, the sudden silence reminding her why she'd woken up. 'Oops.' Her fingers finally closed around the phone and pulling it out she checked to see who'd called in case it was an emergency. 'Lissie, which probably means Riley wants to talk to me.' Sort of urgent. 'It must be getting late. Sorry, but I'm going to call him back.'

'Go ahead.' He widened his smile. 'Say hi from me.'

Picking up a pillow, she banged him over the head. 'Sure thing.'

'Mummy, I want to come home. Now,' Riley

told her when Lissie handed him the phone. 'I want to see you.'

Rachel heard the tears threatening in his voice and her heart twisted. He wasn't used to being away from her overnight, but he had wanted to spend the night with Lissie's boys. 'Okay, sweetheart. I'll come and get you shortly. Have you been having fun?'

'Yes, but I'm homesick now.'

'While you're waiting for me, think about what you want to do today. It's Saturday so I'm not working and you don't have to go to Lanette's.'

'I want to go swimming with Ben.' No thinking needed, then.

'You can ask him when you get home.' She glanced at Ben, saw him frown. 'Can I talk to Lissie again?'

'Rachel, I'm sorry it's so early but Riley had started to fret for you, and I know you're usually awake by now,' Lissie told her.

How early? She glanced at her watch still on her wrist. 'Six-twenty. I hadn't realised.'

Lissie gasped. 'Oh, my God. Did you see Ben?

As in go out? A late night, was it? That's why you slept in.' She gasped again. 'You did go home, didn't you? Come on, tell me all.'

Rachel gulped down a comment. 'I'll be there in a few minutes.' She tried to sound stern but suspected she'd failed miserably when Ben grinned at her.

At the other end of the line Lissie roared with laughter. 'Don't come that tone with me, girl. I know you a lot better than that. If you need more time I'll try to keep Riley occupied. He's looking happier already having talked to you.'

'Not necessary. See you shortly.' Rachel snapped the phone shut on Lissie's laughter, and glanced at Ben. 'Sometimes girlfriends are a pain.'

'Don't know. I haven't got one.' Ben leapt out of bed quickly as he saw her going for the pillow again. 'Since the cat's out of the bag with Lissie, why don't I come with you to pick up Riley and we can go swimming then head into town for breakfast?'

'You don't mind that Lissie knows?' She'd expected him to run a mile. Which on this tiny island only brought him right back to where he was now.

Ben lifted her chin with a finger. 'I'm not ashamed of spending the night with you, Rachel. Are you saying you're feeling that way?'

Kissing his finger, she told him, 'Not at all. If I'd thought I'd feel that way I'd never have gone out with you.' The tension around his mouth disappeared. 'Let me go get our swimming gear. I'll meet you outside in ten.'

She stood and snatched up her clothes, shoving arms and legs into the appropriate openings. If she didn't get out of there immediately, that naked body standing in front of her would distract her again, then she'd be very late picking up Riley. Which would only give Lissie more ammunition to tease her with.

Lissie and Pita and the boys thought the swim and breakfast idea a winner and joined them at the beach. As Rachel let her short skirt drop at her feet she felt Ben's eyes on her. When she met his gaze he winked and licked his lips, before whipping around and tossing Riley in the air and catching him.

Riley shrieked with delight. 'Do it again. Do it again.'

Ben obliged before hooking Riley over his shoulder in a fireman's grip and heading down the beach. 'I'll toss you in the water and you have to swim back to shore.'

Rachel watched as Riley eagerly showed off his swimming prowess. She also noted how Ben kept his attention on Riley until he was standing in shallow water.

'So,' said Lissie from beside her. 'Nothing you can say will ever make me think that you weren't spending the night getting up close and personal with Ben.'

Rachel spun around to face her friend. 'Lissie—'

Lissie started to laugh. 'It's written all over your face.' Her laughter grew. 'You look…happy. Plain and simple. Happy. Haven't seen that in ages.'

'Lissie.' Rachel forced annoyance into her voice. 'Listen to me—'

But Lissie was having none of it, and talked through her laughter. 'We're best friends, right? You can't lie to me. Actually, even if you did, the shine in your eyes is a dead giveaway. Just tell me you had a good time.'

Rachel shook her head at Lissie, but began smiling. The same smile she'd worn when she'd woken up. Laughter began rolling up in her throat. 'Yes, I had a darned good time.' And her laughter spilled out, joining Lissie's.

At the water's edge Ben and Pita glanced over at them, then at each other, shaking their heads. Women. Who could understand them? They mightn't have said the words but Rachel could read their faces. And she didn't care. Lissie was right. She was very happy.

Who knew what was ahead for her and Ben? At this particular moment she didn't want to know, didn't need to find out. She would make the most of the time she spent with him. After that, she'd wait and see.

'Mummy, I want to go to school.' Riley dropped his knife and fork, pushed his dinner aside. Then he glowered at her with a frown so tight his eyebrows almost joined together.

Rachel's heart rolled. Jamie used to do that whenever he wanted a serious talk with her. 'You're not five for nearly three months.'

'So? Harry's going next week.'

'Harry's five today. That's why you're going to his party.' It had been a week since the early-morning swim with Ben, and Lissie's family. Riley had been flexing his mental muscles a bit since then, as though he'd gained even more confidence after overnighting away from her. 'To go to school you have to be five.'

'Why?'

'That's just how it is.'

'Why?' demanded Riley.

'Because the headmistress says so and it's her school. Now, eat your dinner.' Rachel pushed his plate back.

'No. I want to go to school.'

'Boys who go to school always eat their dinner.'

'I don't like it.' His bottom lip protruded.

'Fish and chips? You loved them last time.'

'I don't like them tonight.'

'Then I guess it's time for bed, young man.' Rachel pushed her chair back and stood up.

Riley glared at her defiantly. 'I'm not going to bed. It's too early.'

Why did he become belligerent on days she couldn't handle it with aplomb? 'Dinner or bed. Your choice, my man.' And she began clearing up the kitchen. If Riley got down from the table and headed outside to play she wasn't sure what she'd do. Not about to manhandle him back to the table, or to bed, she'd run out of options.

Knock, knock. 'Can I come in?' Ben called from the open front door.

'Yes,' yelled Riley as he leapt down from the table. 'Ben, can we play soccer before it gets dark?'

'Riley, get back here. Now.' Rachel slapped the dishcloth on the bench and turned to come face-to-face with Ben.

'Problem?' he asked quietly.

She nodded. 'The boundaries are being pushed and I'm too tired to cope.'

Ben looked around the kitchen, taking in the

half-eaten meal and Riley's empty chair. 'Hey, Riley, is that fish and chips you've got for dinner?'

Riley paused, hands on hips. 'I don't want them. Come on, Ben. It will be dark soon.'

'Sorry, kid, I can't play tonight.' Ben pulled out a chair and sat down.

'Why not?'

'Because my star player hasn't finished his dinner.'

'I'm not hungry.'

'It's not about what you want, but what you need.' Ben placed his elbows on the table and leant his chin on his entwined hands.

Riley's little brow furrowed as he tried to work out whether this was a trick or not. 'What do you mean?'

'Kid, if you don't eat you'll stop growing.' Ben shook his head. 'I reckon you've grown two inches since I met you. You're going to be a tall guy, but only if you eat all the food your mother gives you.'

Riley regarded Ben as though he sensed a scam

but finally climbed onto his chair. When Ben pushed the plate towards him he picked up his cutlery and cut off a piece of fish to shove in his mouth.

Rachel relaxed, and whispered around a yawn to Ben, 'Thank you.'

'Not a problem. Now, why are you tired?'

'Haven't a clue. Probably the heat, a busy clinic, and lack of sleep in the weekend.' Not to mention having Ben in her bed every night since that first wonderful night they'd made love.

'Wonder why that was.'

'Smirking doesn't suit you,' she snipped. 'Want a coffee?'

'What I want and what I get offered,' Ben snipped straight back. 'I'd love a coffee after soccer practice with my young star.'

With that Riley shoved his plate aside again and charged outside. 'Come on, Ben. Hurry, before the sun goes to sleep.'

Rachel picked up the plate. 'At least he ate most of it.'

Ben dropped a soft kiss on her neck. 'Want

some more sexercise tonight? Or would you prefer a cuddle and a deep sleep?'

Who'd have thought he'd be so considerate? Especially considering the moment he came within a mile of her he got a hard-on. Swallowing a yawn, she smiled. 'I'm afraid I'm greedy.'

'Exercise and sleep, right?' He chuckled as he headed for the yard.

She propped a hip against the bench, fighting the urge to sit down, knowing she'd never get up again if she did, and she had dishes to do, Riley's lunch to make for tomorrow. Effie would scold her for doing the dishes but she still struggled with walking away from her own messes. So, turn around and fill the sink.

Rachel stayed exactly where she was. Shrill, young laughter mingled with deep, booming shouts out on the front lawn. Ben. Already he meant so much to her. Which was scary. She didn't know what her long-term plans were but they didn't involve staying in the Cook Islands for ever. This was a stopgap, a place to recover, to regain the strength she'd lost, to help her son understand that life did keep going and that he could have good, fun times again without feeling bad about them.

The same applied to her. And Ben had helped a lot already. He'd given her tenderness. He'd given her great sex and with that had rebuilt her confidence. He'd given her a sense of belonging in this foreign place by helping her settle in without taking over.

The islanders had swamped her with enthusiasm, their generosity and affection. She loved them all and appreciated everything they did for her, but at times she felt stifled. Lissie had warned her, said it was in their blood to be so caring about visitors. Rachel was a visitor to this place and even if she lived here fifty years that wouldn't change. She might become their favourite guest, but she'd never be a local.

Neither would Ben. Not that it made any difference to how he went about his duties as a policeman, how he spent time coaching the boys on the rugby field, who he mixed with socially.

Ben belonged here, and yet he was still, and always would be, a Kiwi.

On the table her phone vibrated, just as Ben came racing inside, shoving his cellphone into his back pocket. As she flipped the phone open to read her message he said, 'I've got to go. There's an emergency.' He noticed the phone in her hand. 'You're probably being put on standby at the hospital.'

'What's happened?' But Ben had gone, like a tornado, spinning into her kitchen to tell her he was leaving and spinning back out, all within seconds. She read the message in her hand. Men on reef. Possible drowning or multiple injuries. Need all doctors at ED. Her heart plummeted. If it was the reef on the far side of the lagoon, what chance did those men have of surviving? She'd seen how high the breakers rose before hurling down on the rocks. Nothing, nobody could survive the pounding if caught up in that tumultuous water.

'Mum, Ben put the police lights on when he drived away.'

'Drove away,' Rachel automatically corrected. 'I'm going to call Molly to come and spend the night with you. Is that okay?' *Mistake. Don't ask. Tell him you're needed.* 'Some people have been hurt and I have to go to the hospital to make them better.'

'That's okay, Mummy. I know doctors are special people.'

Where had that come from? 'Thanks.'

'Ben said you do important work at the hospital.'

Ben said that? To her boy? Wow.

The phone rang. Lissie. 'You got the message about the accident on the reef?'

'I'll be heading in shortly. Want me to pick you up on my way past?' Rachel asked.

'Please, and bring Riley. He can stay the night here. Lanette's coming over in a minute.'

Sorted. As easily as that. 'I'll pack his clothes for tomorrow.'

'Don't rush. It's going to take some time before they get those idiots off the reef.' Anger laced Lissie's voice.

Shocked, Rachel spluttered, 'What do you mean, idiots?'

'Three tourists, here for a wedding, decided in a drunken moment of stupidity to borrow a boat and circumnavigate the island. No thought to the men who owned the boat and now have no way of making a living. They obviously went too close to the reef and got tugged into the breakers.'

An icy chill settled on Rachel's skin. Ben was going out to those breakers. Would he be safe? Would he be sensible and not charge in carelessly, hell-bent on being a hero by saving those men? Already regarded a hero by the locals, how could he resist proving once again he had the gumption to leap in to drag a man to safety?

Rachel's stomach dropped. Hero Ben to the scene. 'Ben got called out. He left ten minutes ago.'

'So did Pita, with his boat.' Lissie's anger increased. Driven by fear for her husband?

'Pita will be careful, Lis. He won't do anything to jeopardise himself when he's got you and the kids to think of.'

'I know, but it still makes me mad. Those idiots on the reef didn't consider anyone else. How are their families and friends feeling right now? What about the couple who are getting married tomorrow? They'll have put so much effort into organising their big day and their stupid best man has just gone and ruined everything for them,' Lissie vented.

Rachel listened, trying to ignore the panic building at the thought of Ben somewhere out there on that dangerous reef. *Just this once, please be sensible and safe. I've already lost one man in our lives because he was a hero. I can't lose another.*

CHAPTER NINE

'THIS one was unconscious when we hauled his butt off the reef,' Ben told the group of doctors and nurses waiting in the tiny emergency department.

Rachel quashed the relief pouring through her at the sight of a sopping-wet but uninjured Ben. If he'd been the hero out there, at least he'd been a safe one. Today.

Ben was still talking. 'He came round fifteen minutes ago but he's not in good nick. Left arm and leg appear fractured, and there're deep lacerations to his thighs and upper torso.'

Rachel noted the thick wads of bandages on the man's body, presumably to slow bleeding. She listened as Ben went on to give a detailed, very medical description of the young man's situation. The words he used weren't those of a layman.

She thought back to the day he'd asked her about her first clinic and how she'd been surprised at his level of understanding of what she'd told him.

'Rachel, Lissie, this one's yours.' The ED superintendant spoke above the noise of a suddenly active department.

Rachel followed Lissie as their patient was pushed through to Resus by an orderly. The patient might've recovered consciousness but there was no guarantee he wouldn't lose it again. Head injuries were difficult to deal with, especially when there wasn't state-of-the-art equipment to monitor them.

Behind her she could hear Ben giving details about the second patient to be brought in. 'We had to resuscitate him when we got him on board. A fair amount of water was ejected from his lungs. Unfortunately we had to haul him through the water to the boat as it was too risky to take the boat onto the reef. According to his pal, he lost consciousness about ten minutes before we arrived but was breathing for most of that time.'

One of the orderlies asked, 'Were you the one who went into the water to get him?'

'Four of us did.'

'Figured you'd be right in the thick of it.'

Rachel peeked over her shoulder at Ben, seeing how he took this accolade. If anything, he looked uncomfortable, not pumping out his chest as she'd have expected. As Jamie would've done. 'Wasn't there a third man in that boat?' she asked quietly.

His eyes filled with a bleakness that made her shiver. 'The men are still searching. It's pitch dark out there tonight now the rain's started.'

Crossing the room, she reached a hand to him, touched his forearm, squeezed gently. 'That doesn't look good. At least the sea is warm.' Not like the Atlantic.

'That's about the only plus.' Ben put his hand over hers for a moment. 'I'll catch up with you later. I'm heading back out to join the search party.'

'Do you have to? Aren't there plenty of other men already there?'

'It's my job, Rachel. But more than that, I could never walk away from someone in trouble.'

'Look at you. You're soaked. Why don't you change into dry clothes first?'

'The guy who's missing will have been wet through for hours so the sooner we find him the better.' Ben raised his eyebrow at her. 'Besides, I told you, it's raining.'

She wanted to stop him, to hold on and hug him, to tell him not to do anything stupid, but he wasn't going to listen. Knowing that didn't prevent the words that spilled out of her mouth. 'So you'll rush out into the water, regardless of your own safety. Never mind anyone else, never mind the people who care about you. Like a damned hero.'

'Back off, Doc.'

She shrugged. 'Sure. You won't take any notice, anyway.'

Ben stepped close and leaned near so that only she heard the anger in his voice. 'It's not your place to be talking to me like this, Doc.'

That hurt. Talk about being put in her place. So

she wasn't meant to care what happened to him. Fair enough. Another timely warning. Of course, she'd ignored the last one. Her eyes moistened and she blinked rapidly. By being obtuse Ben had just saved her heart. It wasn't too late to call off what they had going between them. Sex between friends. Except, even as she watched him stalk out of the department, she knew he'd become far more than a friend. Just what, she refused to contemplate. Huffing out the breath she hadn't known she held she turned to follow her patient.

The orderly who'd called Ben a hero approached her.

'We all need heroes in our lives. People round here admire Ben for what he does for us. He never puts himself first, always jumping in to help out, to save someone. He never falters.'

'Exactly my point. Stubborn and foolish.'

'Drop it, Rachel.' Ben spoke from the doorway.

Had she really said that out loud? That was going too far, talking about Ben like that in front of the staff. Bad behaviour on her part. Reluctantly Rachel turned to face Ben, her gaze meeting his. Amazingly she read empathy, not anger, in those piercing eyes. Did he really understand why she felt like this? Did it matter if he did or not? She wasn't carrying on with him any more. She'd got too close to him and was already paying the price. He'd break her heart one way or another. If her heart had even got itself back together in the first place.

Half an hour later Lissie tapped the X-ray she was studying. 'We're going to have to operate to pin that thigh.'

'The patient's concussed,' Rachel added.

'But before surgery I'm going to talk to the friends waiting outside.' Lissie talked right over her. 'They're kicking up a stink about wanting their mates flown home to New Zealand. Our hospital facilities aren't what they're used to. Never mind that we're damned fine doctors.' She ground her teeth. 'If they hadn't been so stupid, they wouldn't need the hospital in the first place.'

'Is that normal? To send tourists home in these situations?' Rachel asked.

'More often than not if the injuries are serious.

But we don't lay on special flights unless it's life-and-death. These guys will go on a regular flight tomorrow. So we'll do what we can for them in the meantime. After I've talked to those idiots making a racket in the waiting room.'

'Want me to assist in Theatre?'

'Definitely.' Lissie walked away, back ramrod straight.

Rachel gave instructions to the nurses before heading to scrub up. No sign of Ben or the third man. Despair gripped her. The situation wasn't looking good. No matter that the young men had behaved stupidly—they didn't deserve to pay the ultimate price. If everyone who did something dumb died, the world's population would be in danger of disappearing completely.

Which didn't stop her desperate need for Ben not to leap into the churning waters without being attached to a lifeline and the other men on the boat watching out for him.

In Theatre Rachel got to watch Lissie at work for the first time. 'You're good at this.'

'I'm getting plenty of practice. Being a general surgeon in the Cooks means dealing with a wider range of operations than I had in London. Not that we get lots of fractured femurs here.'

'Are you going to use an intramedullary rod?' Rachel referred to the metal rod often placed inside a fractured thigh bone to help with recovery.

'No, I haven't got any rods so I'll use an external fixator.'

'The good old plate-and-screws approach, eh?' Rachel focused on suturing a deep laceration on the man's opposite thigh. 'I haven't done any surgery other than gynaecological ops since my training days and that was more about observing than operating.'

'Stick around here long enough and you'll become proficient at just about every regular kind of op. Especially fixing fractured skulls and lifting pressure on the brain.' Lissie began screwing the metal plate that would hold the bone while it knitted back together.

'You don't get lots of head injuries, surely?'

'Falling coconuts kill three or four people a year. The lucky ones end up in here. Then there are the people who fall off their scooters and hit the kerb head first.'

Rachel grimaced. 'Why isn't it law for people riding scooters to wear helmets at all times?' The law stated that scooter riders had to stay below forty kilometres an hour if they didn't wear a helmet. But even at that speed serious damage could be inflicted on a body if it hit something hard, and there weren't many soft landing places around the island.

'I think Ben's working on that, trying to get it compulsory for all riders and their passengers to wear them.'

Back to Ben. The man of the hour. Not that he seemed to see it that way. Surely that showed he didn't get too big-headed about saving people? Maybe he was just a regular guy who liked helping where he could.

Fifty minutes later they wrapped up. Their patient was as comfortable as they could make him. Tomorrow he'd be flying home, to a hospital full of specialists and every piece of equipment imaginable. 'He's very lucky you're here, Lis.' Rachel yawned, the tiredness she'd forgotten while the emergency had been on having returned.

'Let's grab a coffee.' Lissie yawned too. 'My kids kept me up late last night talking about Harry starting school next week. What's your excuse?'

'Not Riley.' She tried not to repeat her yawn, failed.

Lissie gave her a sudden, unexpected hug. 'Bet a certain black-eyed cop had something to do with it.'

'Didn't you say something about coffee?' Rachel forced a smile, then remembered. 'Riley kicked up a stink at dinner tonight. He wants to begin school with Harry.'

'Why don't you let him? He's not many months shy of turning five and he's a bright boy. Better than him having to get used to spending his days with new kids when he could be with the friends he knows.'

'A very compelling argument. Would the school take him early?' Rachel began to see the benefits.

'Can't see why not. Talk to the head teacher.'

'I will.' Rachel was pleased she'd made a quick decision. Sometimes recently she'd found herself flip-flopping between choices, which was totally unlike her. Becoming an islander?

They drank coffee, checked on their patient, and peered through the glass doors into the torrential rain spilling out of the clouds.

'Think we should phone someone?' Rachel asked. 'What about Pita?' She wasn't about to risk Ben's wrath by calling him.

'Pita hates me interrupting him during a search-and-rescue job. We'll have to sit it out.' Lissie turned for the canteen. 'Want a game of Scrabble?'

'Scrabble? You're thinking you'll beat me because I can hardly keep my eyes open.'

A nurse approached. 'You can stand down now. They've found the third man on the beach. He swam ashore.'

'Any injuries?' Rachel asked.

The nurse shook her head. 'Apparently not. Ben's checked him over and says he's good to go.'

'But Ben's not a doctor.' So how did that explain his medical knowledge? Actually, that's what she'd do when next she saw him. Ask him to explain.

And while you're at it, explain your earlier outburst to him so it doesn't fester between you both.

Ben parked outside his house and flicked the headlights off. Automatically he glanced towards Rachel's place, as he did every single time he arrived home from work, from the pub, from any damned where.

You've got more than the hots for her, Ben, me boy. You're wondering what it would be like to come home to Rachel every day.

Which was why he should be backing off from what they had going between them. Sex was one thing; getting any further involved was another. He shivered. How could he quit when she filled his head every waking moment? When he couldn't keep his hands off her? When had he begun to believe there was more to his future than being a single cop on a remote island in the middle of the Pacific?

Hell, and what happened at the end of Rachel's twelve-month stint here? If she didn't sign on again, would he follow her around the world to wherever she stopped next? No way. That would be madness. He'd made a new life for himself. One that he felt safe in, secure in a lonely kind of way. He had friends here, family who regularly turned up. This is where he belonged now, who he was. It had taken too much effort and hurt to get to this place in his life; he would not forsake it all. He would not chance his heart. Not for Rachel, not for the doc.

Anyway, it wasn't a case of if she didn't stay, but when she'd leave. She might be happy now but she'd soon tire of the laid-back lifestyle and lack of amenities. Most people who came here to work did.

But what if Rachel was different and did adjust to the island way of life permanently? Hope flickered in his chest, died almost immediately.

Ben elbowed open the door of the truck. Outside he stood, mindless of the rain, staring up at the black clouds, his hands gripping his hips.

Anger rolled through him, heated his cold belly. Where had that naïve idea come from? She was a city woman, born and bred, used to having everything at her fingertips. And if she didn't worry for herself about what she was missing out on, she'd soon start thinking about lost opportunities for Riley.

He spun around, skidded on the wet grass, righted himself. Glaring at Rachel's house, he silently shouted at her. *This is all your fault. I never wanted to feel for anyone again. Never, do you understand? But I feel for you, care about what happens to you, and you, damn it, you gave me a bollocking tonight about who I am. Well, it's got to stop.*

He slammed the door, leapt the fence and strode up to her front door where a light burned brightly behind the glass. From now on Rachel was nothing but the doc. Not Rachel, the hot woman next door with eyes that would tempt a monk into breaking his vows of celibacy. Except the boundaries between the doc and Rachel had blurred, rolled into the one whole package that she really was.

His carefully put-together life was tilting, spinning out of control. If he didn't do something to rectify this right now, it would be too late. If it wasn't already. Gawd help him.

Ben lifted his hand to knock, stopped. It was well after midnight and Rachel had been exhausted hours ago at dinnertime. She'd be sound asleep now. So why was the light on? Expecting him? After what she'd mouthed off at him in the hospital? Not likely.

Shrugging away the tension in his shoulders, he turned the door handle and let himself in. Treading purposefully, he headed down the short hallway, peering into the lounge as he passed. Backed up and stood in the doorway to study a sleeping Rachel curled under a light cover.

With her eyes closed her accusations were hidden. She'd said the word 'hero' as though it was poison. Fear had glittered out at him from behind that fury she'd unleashed briefly. Fear of what? Something happening to him? That should've made him feel good, but instead his churning anger grew. Didn't she know him well enough yet to realise he'd never leap into a situation before he'd assessed every aspect? Damn, she knew how to stick a knife in and turn it.

You shouldn't be vulnerable enough to get hurt. You're supposed to be remaining aloof from any entanglement. This is why you didn't want another woman in your life. Women asked too much of their men, expected them to ignore an intrinsic part of their make-up. Even Catrina had made demands on him he hadn't been able to fulfil—like the time she thought he could forego spending Christmas with his family because she'd wanted to spend it with friends. *Yeah, and look at you now. When was the last time you went back to the folks for that particular celebration?* Not since Catrina had died. Huh. He hadn't been willing to give up a family tradition for his wife, but he sure as hell had done it because of her.

And now Rachel had given him grief over rescuing some foolish tourist from the reef. Didn't she know how intrinsic it was for him to save people in jeopardy? He couldn't stop himself any more than he could stop breathing.

His gaze roamed her sleeping form. He knew that body intimately, loved the curves and flat planes. Adored the way her face lit up when she smiled, and how those hungry eyes twinkled with fun and even mischief at times. His anger backed down, replaced with a sense of hopelessness. How could they stop what was going on between them? He crossed to her, leaned down to run a finger over her soft cheek. His heart rolled over with some alien emotion so strong that he froze. He needed her. He cared deeply for her. But no matter how he felt about Rachel, he couldn't carry on.

He could use her outburst of tonight to fuel a break. After all, she had no right to have asked that of him. Why had she? She'd wanted those men rescued as much as anyone had. She just hadn't wanted him to be the rescuer.

No, she didn't want you acting stupid, being a hero.

Because of what her late husband had done. Hadn't she said something about the guy rushing into that warehouse before backup had been in place? He'd seen the despair in Rachel's eyes when she'd talked about her husband's death.

Rachel stirred, rolled onto her back, the cover slipping to the floor.

Ben held his breath but thankfully she didn't wake. She'd have a fit to find him standing here, watching over her. But she needed to be in bed, comfortable, not sleeping out here on that lumpy couch. Without thought he bent and carefully lifted her into his arms. Warm and soft. Smelling of lavender. Filling him with need. Undermining his determination to break off their relationship—if that's what they had.

Against his chest she murmured something in her sleep and he wanted to hold her tight, never let her go. Surely they could face their gremlins together, bury them once and for all? She did that to him. Made him dream again. Made him want things he could never have. Made him believe he might have a full life some time in the future. Until the day she packed up and left. Then where would he be?

'Ben?' she murmured against him, her body tensing.

'Shh, yes, it's me. I'm putting you to bed.'

'Ben.' Her eyes flew wide open. Her sleep-creased mouth spread slowly into a smile. 'Hey, I was waiting for you.' She wriggled to be let down and her feet searched for the floor.

'I should leave.' One look at her and that idea flew out the window. Leaning right into her body, he held her face in his hands, traced her mouth with his finger. 'We need to talk, not make love.' Not what his body was telling him. Not what he was doing.

Her eyes widened, her tongue slid across the tip of his thumb. That simple gesture sent desire storming through his body, reaching out to his fingers, down to his toes, into his chest to make his heart thump hard and loud, through to his manhood, making that throb and stand up. 'To-morrow,' she muttered, then bit his thumb gently.

'Ahh, Rachel, the things you do to me.'

'I haven't done anything. Yet.' Her voice was full of promise.

A promise that he could not ignore, did not have the strength to deny. His hands found her butt, lifted her against him. As her legs wound around him all that desire rolled into a deep groan that blew through his throat and across his tongue. His mouth possessed hers. He kneaded her soft flesh. His brain gave up trying to say stop and went with the rush.

Rachel clung to him as he pressed his erection against her. A hand pushed between them, searching for his zip, tugging it down, releasing him from the constrictions of fabric into her warm hand. A shudder rocked him, turned his legs to water. With aching slowness and yet, at the same time, amazing speed he carried her to the sideboard at the end of the room and sat her on the edge.

He jerked his head back, staring at this siren. His hand caressed her moist flesh. Her bare flesh. When had she removed her panties?

Lifting her head, she looked directly at him, laughter crinkling the corners of her eyes that were full of trust, full of that deep need for him that stole his sanity and drove him deep into her.

'Hurry,' she whispered, not looking away.

'No choice,' he muttered. 'You take me from nothing to everything in no time at all.' He pushed deeper.

A sweet moan slipped over her lips.

He withdrew, filled her again. Another moan, this time sharper. And she tightened around him. Now he could not hold back. Hurry, she'd said. Hurry she'd get.

She still hadn't broken that eye contact. It was as sexy as hell seeing the exact moment she came. All in a blink before he poured his need into her. Then he gathered her against him, held her tight as their bodies shook and cooled, and still he didn't let her go.

He couldn't. Somehow Rachel had melted into him, become a part of him that would take more than a few words to sever. Her lips moved against his neck.

'What?' he whispered, afraid to break the moment.

'You're a wonderful lover,' she said a little louder.

'I'm not on my own there.' A glow of satisfaction covered him. 'That was mind-blowing.'

She wriggled free, stood up and took his hand to drag him along to her bedroom where they curled around each other and started all over again, slowly this time.

Much later Ben rolled over and peered through the gloom at the bedside clock. Two-twenty. *Time flies when you're having fun.* He stretched over the bed. Every muscle ached sweetly. His eyes drooped shut as exhaustion stole over him, along with a deep sense of having found something he couldn't quite put his finger on but knew was right.

'Hey,' Rachel whispered. 'You awake?'

'Yeah. Just.' He rolled onto his side, reached for her and wrapped his body along her back, his arm draped over her waist. 'I should go home. Wouldn't want Riley to find me here in the morning.'

She tensed. 'True. I don't want him getting the wrong idea.'

Ben took his hand away, put some space between their bodies. 'Define "wrong idea".'

'That he might see you as a replacement for his father.'

Relief and disappointment tangled together, tightened his muscles. Didn't she see him as a good role model for a father? He was great with kids. Ask anyone on the island, they'd all stick up for him. *Hang on. What about that sense of relief fighting to come out on top of your emotions right now?*

Why did he feel relieved? Easy. Because she wasn't asking any more of him than what they already had.

Then she blew everything sky-high by saying, 'I was going to tell you I couldn't do this any more.' Her gulp was loud in the suddenly quiet room. 'As if I had a hope of that. You're like a drug, very addictive and not to be denied.'

So she'd had the same thoughts he'd had about their relationship. She'd been intending to call it all off. That stung. Yeah, like it was all right for him to think of doing the same to her. 'I know what you mean.' He struggled upright, sat back against the headboard. Silence fell between them. 'You might be right about us stopping seeing each other except as neighbours and friends.'

Rachel's hand found his, gripped it tight. 'How do we do that when we only have to come within fifty metres of each other and we're falling apart with need?'

He lifted her hand to his lips and kissed the palm, then each finger in turn. 'We're going to have to dig deep, find the strength that's got us both through other crises and move on.'

Then he placed her hand on her thigh and climbed off the bed. He hauled his jeans on and slung his shirt over his shoulder. 'I'll see myself out.'

CHAPTER TEN

'THANK goodness for Sundays.' Rachel shook herself further down into the soft couch in Lissie's lounge. All the glass doors were wide open and they gazed out under the overhanging roof onto the sodden lawn where the boys raced around, soaked to the bone.

'Too many late nights getting the better of you?' Lissie asked with a suggestive grin.

'None at all.' For more than a week. Since the night of the rescue and the steamy conclusion to her relationship with Ben.

He hadn't been at home when she'd ducked across before work to see him the first morning to return his boxers, and for the rest of the week he'd been noticeable by his absence. Occasionally she'd heard him drive up to his front door late at night, but in the morning even at the ghastly hour she woke he'd be gone.

According to Lissie, the police had instigated an investigation into the theft of the boat by the three young men. 'From what I've heard, Ben read the Riot Act to the guy who was lucky not to be injured. He pointed out that a family depended on that boat to make their living, then demanded to know what the men intended doing about reparation.'

Rachel felt her mouth lifting into a smile despite her heavy heart. 'I can see Ben doing that. What was the outcome?'

'They've bought the family a new boat.'

'Strike one to Ben.' But where was he? A whole week without seeing those brooding eyes and feeling his unexpectedly light touch on her skin was a whole week too long.

He had agreed with her that they should pull back from wherever their relationship had been taking them. And now she wished she'd kept her mouth shut. But this enforced break from Ben might be a good thing, give her time to put her feelings for him into perspective.

So why did she feel so droopy and sad? To top

it all off, the rain hadn't stopped since the night of the boating accident. Heavy, warm rain, creating endless puddles, which Riley loved jumping into and getting filthy. It was as though the clouds were stuck above the island and the wind was never going to shift them off. Apparently this was normal for May.

Lissie nudged her. 'Earth to Rachel. You're space-tripping again.'

'Again? What do you mean by that?' Rachel reached for the glass of pawpaw juice.

'I think you've fallen for Ben. Ever since you spent that first night with him you've started going off into these little daydreams.' Lissie laughed.

'Fallen for Ben? No way, absolutely not. I can't, Lis, you know that.' Panic rose in her throat. It was one thing to suspect she might have, but for Lissie to be voicing the same conclusion really brought the truth crashing home. Plus all the complications that came with that truth.

Lissie tucked her legs up on the couch, looking serenely complacent. 'Why ever not? I know you still miss Jamie but, Rach, it's definitely time to have some fun, don't you think?'

'You said I'd fallen for Ben. That's not about having fun. That's serious.' She sipped her juice, worried she mightn't be able to swallow it if she took too much.

'What are you afraid of?'

That was easy. 'Everything.'

Her friend merely smiled at her. 'Wrong. You've got the having-sex-with-someone-new issue out of the way. If the glow in your eyes lately is an indicator, that went more than well.'

The juice was sweet and rich on her tongue, and her throat worked fine. 'No complaints there.'

'So stop worrying about the rest. Take things one day at a time. Enjoy doing what you already do together—the swimming, eating out, the fun.' She paused and grinned. 'Get to know each other beyond the heat and passion. You've already found the sense of belonging together.'

'How do you know that's how I feel?' Was there anything Lissie hadn't figured out?

'You're an easy read.'

'Thanks a bunch.' Rachel twisted her glass around in her fingers. 'I haven't seen Ben for a week. He seems to have made himself unavailable. There was a note on the door a few nights back to say he wouldn't be able to play ball with Riley for a while as he was tied up at work. Doing what? Here, in the islands where Ben told me nothing happens?'

Lissie placed her glass on the coffee table and stood up. 'I think we need something a little stronger than juice.' At the liquor cabinet she pushed aside bottles to reach into the back. 'Here we go. I'm going to make margaritas.'

Rachel stared at Lissie as memories of other nights on cocktails flooded her head. She forced her tone to sound grave. 'This spells trouble. I'll have you know my son's out there and I have to remain responsible and sensible.' Then spoilt the whole thing by chuckling.

'Good, you can look out for my kids too.' Lissie began measuring tequila into a cocktail shaker. 'Seriously, Pita's in the shed, already watching out for them. There's nothing to worry about.'

She twisted the top off the bottle of orange liqueur. 'I haven't had one of these since London. What have I been doing with my life?'

'Interfering in mine too much.' Rachel drained her juice and sat back, giving in to the inevitable. There was no stopping Lis when she made her mind up to do something and, anyway, Rachel didn't feel like sitting by and watching her friend enjoying their favourite cocktail alone.

The first icy sip was delicious. Rachel tipped the salt-encrusted rim of the glass to her lips again. 'If you ever get sick of being a doctor you've got another career option right here.' She held the cocktail aloft. 'Actually, you could combine both. This has to be the cure for just about anything that ails people.'

'I aim to please. Now you're staying for dinner. We're having barbequed chicken.'

'Yes, ma'am.' Rachel made herself even more comfortable on the sofa, happy to relax and put the issue of Ben aside for a while.

Lissie asked, 'Have you got everything ready for Riley's first day at school?'

'And some. He's so excited. Tomorrow can't come fast enough. We've bought new shorts and a shirt, which Effie's ironed already. They're lying on the spare bed along with pens, pencils, a pad and a ruler. Riley checks them over about once an hour.' He might drive her crazy with the continuous ritual but to see him so thrilled about starting school more than made up for it.

'Hey, am I late?' Ben drawled.

Rachel sat up straight, blinking at the apparition standing in the doorway. She turned to Lissie. 'Late for what?'

'The barbeque, of course. Didn't I—?' Lissie smacked her forehead. 'No, I didn't.'

Rachel glared at her. 'Thanks, pal.' But at least she'd get to see Ben a bit, and maybe even talk to him about last week.

'I'll go find Pita. Is he out in his shed?' Ben asked. He beat a hasty retreat before Lissie had a chance to answer.

'You'd better have a good reason for not warning me.' Rachel kept her glare in place.

'How about I didn't want you leaving if you knew Ben was coming?'

'Why would I? I'm not avoiding him. It's the other way round.' Another thought crossed her mind. 'Did Ben know I'd be here?'

'I think Pita told him.' But Lissie didn't look at Rachel. 'It doesn't matter. You're both here and we'll have a great night.'

'I hope you know what you're doing.' Because Rachel was getting very confused with her own need to see Ben and the knowledge that she shouldn't.

'Chill. Want another margarita?'

She mustn't. Not with Ben out there. What if the alcohol got the better of her tongue and she said something else to upset Ben? What the heck? Live dangerously. 'Yes, please.'

Too late. Lissie was already shaking the life out of the cocktail mixer.

Watching Riley chasing the soccer ball through the mud and puddles, Ben's chest expanded. The kid had to be the noisiest being on earth. His shrieks of excitement went on and on. What had happened to that sad little boy who'd mistaken him for his dad?

Dad. Ben sucked a lungful. Dad. What was it like to be called 'Daddy'? To have a kid hug him goodnight? To rush out to greet him, yapping on about his day? *Like Riley already does with you.*

'Hold this while I tighten the bolts, will you?' Pita dropped a spanner on the cart's engine hood, making a hell of a racket. 'Darn.'

Riley lined up the ball and the makeshift goal-posts, swung his leg back, and gave it all his little body had. The ball slid across the mud into the left-hand post and spun away. The kid sprang after it, laughing. 'Did you see that, Ben?'

'Yeah, kid, I did. Way to go.'

'You going to stand there all day?' Pita nudged him. 'A bloke could do with a hand here.'

Ben grinned. 'Sure. I can't wait to see those guys riding around on this cart.' Already he could picture Riley's face split into the biggest grin ever.

'You told Rachel about this project yet?'

Ouch. 'Ahh, no.'

Pita thumped Ben's back. 'You'd better, mate. She'll kill you if you don't ask if it's okay for Riley to drive a go-cart that goes at least fifteen k's an hour.'

'What if she says no? It's not like she'd understand what boys love doing. Bet she didn't have a cart while growing up in London.' This was where Riley's dad would've stepped in for the kid. But Jamie wasn't here to do that. Ben felt that squeezing sensation in his chest again. It mightn't be his place but he'd have to explain to Rachel that boys had to be boys, and that bumps and bruises were all part of growing up.

'Hold that bonnet straight, will you?' Pita began tightening bolts. 'Rachel doesn't tend to namby-pamby Riley. I'm sure you can convince her it's a good idea. Once my boys have been riding on the cart, there's no way she'll have any hope of stopping Riley hopping on and riding around the block, anyway.'

'Riley? Ride a go-cart? Where?' Rachel's eyes widened in that endearing manner she had that could also be a storm warning. 'It's not like there's a lot space here to ride round.'

They were sitting on the deck after dinner, the men drinking beer, the girls coffee. Ben had hoped to talk about this later but Harry and Jason had beaten him to it. At least Rachel had waited until all the boys had gone inside to watch TV.

Ben chugged a mouthful of beer, placed the bottle carefully on the table and told her, 'There's the reserve just along the road. And the kids can use the back roads when we're around to supervise them.'

'Back roads? You've got to be kidding me.' Rachel spluttered into her coffee mug. 'How fast will that thing go?'

'We've jammed the gear in second so probably about fifteen k's an hour, maybe a wee bit more.' Ben winced as he watched her eyes get even bigger. Should he duck now? Or take her wrath like a man?

But Rachel turned to Lissie. 'You're happy with this?'

Lissie nodded. 'The project wouldn't even have started if I hadn't been.'

'Boy stuff, isn't it?' Rachel nibbled her fingernail. 'I'll worry like crazy the whole time I know Riley's on that thing but—' she shrugged '—okay, I can't be an ogre and say no when his friends will be riding around and telling him what a fantastic time they're having.'

Relief relaxed Ben. Rachel had the power to surprise him. 'The boys will have to wear helmets or no ride. They cannot take the cart off Pita's yard if no parents are around.'

'How come you're the one setting all the rules?'

When he wasn't one of the parents. Ben heard that loud and clear, and tried not to let it upset him. Rachel had a point. He wasn't a parent to any of these kids. But 'I'm a cop, and certain things like safety come first.'

And I damned well care about these kids, especially about your boy. I'm looking out for him as his dad would've done.

Which meant he was in big trouble. The kid's mum had crept under his skin when he'd thought he'd had himself totally under control. Now it looked like the kid himself had sneaked into his heart too. Face it, both of them had touched him emotionally right from the get-go. When Riley had turned those suck-you-in eyes on him that first night and asked if he was Daddy, Ben had felt as though a steamroller had flattened him. And Rachel's gaze had buried him under a ton of need and lust and responsibility and love.

Love. There was that word again. It popped up unbidden so often now he was beginning to believe it, feel it, taste it. This was when he should run. Down the road, along the beach, anywhere as long as he headed away from Rachel and her boy.

Rachel yawned. 'Time to go home, I think. Those boys have gone awfully quiet.'

Ben stood up. 'I'll drive you home.' And when Rachel blinked up at him he added, 'You've been drinking.' She wasn't used to alcohol and her two cocktails added up to more than his two beers. What had happened to running away? He shrugged. He was done running. What ever happened in the future, running was no longer an option. It hadn't worked, anyway. He'd come home exhausted, sore and still confused. And in love.

Settling a sleeping Riley on the back seat, Ben buckled the seat belt while Rachel collected her medical bag from the car. He ran the back of his hand down the kid's cheek. A surge of tenderness swamped him, leaving him momentarily breathless. He backed away, straightened and looked over the truck roof right into the eyes that haunted his dreams.

'Ready to go?' he growled when her lips curved upwards.

'More than.' Rachel slid into the front passenger seat. 'You're good with Riley.'

'It's not hard. He's a great kid.'

Rachel peered through the windscreen. 'Will it ever stop raining again? I've been going stir-crazy shut inside all the time.'

'Then get out. It's only water. Not even cold.' So she wasn't happy. Step one in the process of coming around to thinking about her next move at the end of her contract. It had been hard enough staying away from her all week; how would he cope if she left permanently?

The engine roared to life. The truck bounced as he backed quickly down the drive onto the road. The sooner they were home the sooner he could find peace and quiet on his front deck.

They didn't get far. Around the second corner Ben braked hard to avoid driving into a crowd of people surrounding one of the buses that took tourists to and from the cultural show.

'Has there been an accident?' Rachel peered through the dark.

'If there has, it's very recent. No cops around to keep people off the road and out of further danger.' Ben pushed out of the vehicle. 'Will Riley be all right in there while we take a look?'

'He won't wake now. Believe me.' Rachel quickly followed him as he pushed through the onlookers to the front of the bus.

Ben swore quietly. Two young people lay on the edge of the road, their bodies twisted and torn. Turning, he held his hands up to still the excited chatter of the crowd. 'Step back, people. The doc needs room to attend to these two. Has anyone called the police yet? Or the hospital?'

As he heard the affirmative replies Ben sighed thankfully. At least someone had used their noggin sensibly. 'Right, everyone get off the road.' As the crowd started muttering and grumbling he roared, 'There's still traffic out and about, and it's dark in this rain so move along. Do any of you want to be the next person hit?' Not waiting for an answer, he knelt down beside the victims, then looked up again. 'What happened? Does anyone know?'

'They were walking along the side of the road as we were coming along,' a woman told him. 'A dog shot across in front of the bus and the driver swerved. There was an awful thump. Must've been when the bus hit these two.'

'Thanks, lady. Would you mind waiting until a policeman arrives so you can give him your statement?' Ben flipped open his cellphone and pressed speed dial. 'Hey, Tetevano, have you heard there's been an accident round by Fruit of the Island? Good. Right. See you shortly.'

Rachel hunkered down beside him. 'I need to warn Lissie.' She pressed her phone to her ear.

Ben told her, 'Hospital's been alerted. The ambulance is coming, but that doesn't mean paramedics. You're it until we get these two to the hospital.'

In the half-light from the streetlamp he saw the surprise in her eyes. 'You're not giving me a hand with this?'

He sighed. Of course he was. He'd spoken out of habit. 'Want me to see to the young man?'

'Please. Help yourself to anything in the bag. Let me know if I have to administer drugs.' While filling Lissie in on the situation, Rachel studied the girl sprawled on the gravel, who was looking dazed and unfocused.

The young man in front of Ben groaned and tried to roll onto his side. 'Take it easy, buddy. You've been in an accident. I don't want you moving until I've checked you over, okay?'

'Where's Ellie? She was with me. What happened?' The guy continued trying to push himself upright.

'Ellie's beside you. What's your name?' Ben gently pushed the guy down again, began counting his respiratory rate before taking a pulse.

'My head hurts.'

Probably from slamming onto the road. Ben's fingers gently felt all over the skull. 'Your name, buddy?'

'Thomas. Ouch.'

Ben's fingers had found a soft spot on the side of the guy's jaw. 'Take it easy. You've got a massive bruise here.' Hopefully that's all it was. At least the guy's speech was clear so the jaw was moving properly and probably not broken.

A metre away Rachel said, 'Ellie, leave your face alone, please. I'll give you something for the pain but best we wait until you're in hospital where I can see clearly before we start removing the gravel from your cheek. But first I need to check you over. Do you hurt anywhere else?'

A scream rent the air, sending shivers down Ben's spine. The girl was scratching at her face, ignoring Rachel's pleas to stop. Ben crossed to help Rachel, taking the girl's hands and holding them away from her face so she couldn't cause any more damage. When Ellie began kicking out with her feet as she attempted to break free of him, Ben looked around, saw Tetevano coming through the crowd. 'Tete, give us a hand, will you?'

Tetevano instantly assessed the problem and knelt to grip Ellie's ankles while Rachel administered a shot of morphine. 'Thanks. Hopefully the drug will calm her as it holds the pain in abeyance.'

Ben continued to hold Ellie's hands while Rachel made her survey, looking at and feeling each of Ellie's limbs, her abdomen, her head. 'Gash on the forehead needs stitches. One knee is twisted but I don't think it's more than a sprain. A lot of skin missing but otherwise I think this young lady has come off quite lightly. I can't find where the bus hit her.'

'Maybe she was bumped aside by Thomas when the bus hit him.' Ben left Ellie, now that she'd quietened down, to return to his patient, who'd slumped sideways. 'Hey, Thomas.'

Rachel joined them, and together they went through the routine of checking the man out. Ben was surprised how easily everything came back to him. It was as though he'd never been away from medicine. Was he really meant to be a doctor after all? No. No way. It was one thing to know what he was doing when he had someone as capable as Rachel on hand, quite another to be in the field on his own, dealing with an emergency.

They heard the siren long before the ambulance reached them. Most people had gone, the rain too much of a deterrent to standing around watching ghoulishly.

'You go with them, Rachel, in case you're needed. I'll take Riley home and tuck him into bed.'

'Why don't you go with the ambulance?' She blinked away raindrops as she stared at him. 'We both know you're qualified to.'

'It's your job, not mine.' And he turned away

before he saw all the questions in her eyes that would most certainly be racing through her mind right at that moment. The last thing he needed was Rachel feeling sorry for him.

CHAPTER ELEVEN

AFTER getting up at six-thirty on Monday morning in great anticipation of his first day at school, Riley was dressed and ready to go by seven.

'Sit back at the table and eat your cereal.' Rachel tried to sound stern but couldn't keep a straight face.

'I ate some.' He shoved the plate sideways and it spun dangerously close to the edge of the table.

'If that goes on the floor, you'll be cleaning up the mess, young man. You don't want to get your school clothes dirty, do you?'

'Why can't I go to school now?'

'Because it's too early. No one will be there for at least another hour.' Rachel pointed to the clock. 'What time does that say?'

Riley's nose screwed up as he concentrated on the green digital figures. 'Seven-one-two.'

'Right. You have to wait until it says eight-oh-oh. Then we'll drive along to the gate and wait for Lissie's boys. Okay?'

'I can't wait that long, Mummy. That's for ever.' Riley pulled his plate back across the table with a scraping noise that set Rachel's nerves on end.

After the drama of the accident between the bus and the two young tourists she'd had little sleep. It had been late when she'd finally got home, and Ben, who'd been waiting on her porch, had immediately headed for the fence and his place, saying nothing more than goodnight. Was he avoiding talking to her in case she asked about his medical background? At twelve-thirty in the morning he didn't need an excuse—it was not really the hour to have in-depth conversations.

'What's for my lunch?' Riley demanded.

Pleasure tugged at her, lifting her spirits. The first-ever school morning and the question that he'd probably ask her every day until he was past taking home-made lunches. 'It's a surprise. Your favourite things.'

'Did you like school, Mummy?'

'Yes, I did.' Not a lot. Rachel poured a coffee and spread her toast with honey. 'You'll make lots of friends.' Please. School wasn't such a nice place for the kids who didn't, as she well knew. 'Then there're all the books to read, and sums to learn, and lots of other things the teachers will show you.'

'Will they want to know what I'm going to be when I grow up?'

'Not yet. What do you want to be?' She could've added *this week* but bit into her toast instead.

'A policeman, like Ben.'

Half-chewed toast lodged in Rachel's throat. She coughed and coughed, finally dislodging it. Washing it down with a mouthful of coffee, she took a deep breath and asked, 'What happened to being a pilot?'

'I like policemen. Like Daddy and Ben.'

Please let this phase pass quickly. Following in the footsteps of Jamie and Ben didn't bode well for her peace of mind in years to come. 'Okay.'

'And I'd like a police dog. I saw one on TV last night.'

Eight o'clock finally arrived and Riley followed her around the house as she gathered up keys, handbag, lunch and a stack of patient files.

'Patience, Riley. The school won't run away without you.'

'What if the teachers don't know I'm coming and start without me?'

'They know. I promise.' She pointed outside to the sky. 'See, even the sun is celebrating your day.' Thank goodness. There was a stack of washing that needed drying and the house felt damp all the time at the moment.

'Hey, where's the schoolboy?' Effie called from the back door.

'Effie, come in. You're early.' Rachel placed her things on the table and waved a mug in Effie's direction. 'Want a coffee?'

'Thanks, Rachel.' Effie bounced over to Riley and handed him a parcel wrapped in cotton cloth with a hibiscus flower tucked into a fold. 'For your first day at school.'

Riley's eyes widened. 'Thank you, Effie. Can I open it now?'

'You'd better. You might need it today.'

Effie hadn't finished talking when Riley had the wrapping off a blue plastic lunch box with silver stars stuck to the top. 'Wow, Effie, that's cool. I haven't got a lunch box. Mummy, look.'

Effie gave him a quick hug. 'You do now. Shall I put your sandwich and biscuits in it?'

Rachel gave Effie a smile and handed her the coffee. 'That's lovely. You're spoiling him.'

'Why not? He's a great kid.'

'Mummy, can we go now?'

'I guess we'd better. Effie, take it easy today, eh? I don't need anything done until the washing dries, and then I can bring that in and fold it when I get home.'

Effie shook her head. 'You go to school and then work. I'll just do a quick flick around.'

Which meant Effie would be busy for hours, polishing already gleaming surfaces, scrubbing clean floors even cleaner. 'You're spoiling me too.'

Tossing everything on the back seat, Rachel climbed into the car, glancing across at Ben's house as she did every morning. No sign of him, and his police truck wasn't in the drive. Another early start? As the car rolled down the drive and out onto the road she decided she needed to buy her own vehicle. It was all very well having this freedom to use Ben's car but she shouldn't still be taking advantage of his generosity.

Sadness enveloped her. It amazed her how much she missed Ben. Not only the nights in bed, but the coffees on her deck, the gentle teasing about her inability to swim despite his numerous lessons. Somewhere along the way he'd slipped under her radar and caught her while she'd been looking elsewhere. Lissie had a point. The time to move on from Jamie had well and truly arrived. Crikey, she was already halfway down the track if the way her heart squeezed every time she saw or heard Ben was anything to go by.

'Mummy, you've gone past the gate.' Riley shouted in her ear, causing her to jerk the steering wheel.

Lifting her foot from the accelerator, she drove into the nearest driveway to turn around. 'Silly

Mummy.' Even on Riley's special day Ben swamped her mind, taking control of her thought processes, rendering her incapable of something as simple as spotting Lissie's front gate.

The boys stepped into the middle of the road, waving up a storm. Carefully manoeuvring onto the grass verge, Rachel wound down her window. 'Get off the road, you silly billies. What happens if a car comes?'

'We'll shift,' Jason told her seriously. 'Why did you go down to Kepu's house?'

'Mummy was daydreaming.' Riley giggled excitedly as he slipped out of the car and joined his friends.

Rachel shrugged. Even her son could read her these days. 'Where's your mum, boys?'

'In the house, yelling that we made a mess in the kitchen.'

Rachel made her way inside and found Lissie rushing around. 'You look like a demented hen. Want a hand with anything?'

'A spring clean from top to toe wouldn't go amiss.' Lissie slammed a drawer shut and swept breadcrumbs off the table into her hand. 'But I guess that will have to wait.' She looked up and smiled. 'Are you ready for Riley's big morning?'

Sudden moisture blurred Rachel's vision. 'No, yes, maybe.'

'That about covers it.' Lissie gave her a hug. 'You'll be fine.'

'I know. I just wish his dad could see him. He'd be so proud.' Jamie had had big plans for his boy's future. No child of his would be a policeman. At least not without a degree behind him first.

Lissie's arms tightened around her. 'Want me to come with you? I can phone in and say I'll be a wee bit late.'

Lissie had patients booked in from nine. Rachel straightened out of her friend's embrace. 'No, I'll be fine. Promise. I'd better get going before Riley implodes with excitement.'

'My boys aren't much better. They consider Riley as a brother so this is as special a day as Harry's was. I'll come and wish Riley luck.'

Rachel linked arms with Lissie as they walked

to the gate. 'I'm glad you persuaded me to come out here. You've got me through so much in the past and you're still doing it. I should be standing on my own two feet by now.'

'Hey, you are. Admit it, today's a biggie for any parent. I cried when both my boys started school. It's very hard to let them go. They're taking their first step towards becoming independent from us, and we're afraid for them.'

'I guess we don't have children to keep them tied to us for the rest of their lives.' But today Rachel could almost wish for that. Almost. Already Riley was tall for his age, showing that he'd be like his dad when he reached adulthood. And there was no doubting there was a very clever brain in his head.

Ben pulled over outside the school and grimaced as the shrill shrieks of numerous kids playing reached his tender ears. 'Ouch.' Who'd be a teacher?

He glanced towards the front of the building. His heart slowed as he spied Rachel standing there, talking to one of the teachers, Riley's hand firmly in hers. So, the kid was a bit nervous. Starting school was a big deal.

Ben pushed out of the truck and closed the door quietly. He should be heading to town and the station. He most definitely should not be here, looking out for the kid and his mum. But as he'd driven past his foot had come off the accelerator and the truck had slowed. Right. He'd left home early to have breakfast at Swampies, filling in time until now.

If he was honest, he hadn't wanted to miss seeing the kid walk into class for the first time. But starting up the path, his eyes were fixed not on Riley but on Rachel. Her back was so straight it must hurt, her shoulders were taut, and that hand holding Riley's seemed glued to the boy.

This was just as big a day for her. Ben came up behind Rachel and stopped to study her some more. Lavender scent tickled his senses. Those curls that he loved running his fingers through were hooked up in some kind of knot thing with a stick poked through it. He sucked a breath, clenched his fists, fighting the urge to tug the knot undone.

The blood in his veins hummed, sped up. Already he could feel his resolve to stay away from her faltering. Faltering? It had taken a hike, long gone, leaving him with this desperate, gnawing need.

I want Rachel. I want Rachel.

He'd missed her every single second. Did he have the willpower, the strength to continue staying away? Have it or not, he had to or he'd drown in those big eyes and never come back up for air. He'd be a goner. Being in lust was hard enough to deal with, but if that had turned to love, as he suspected, what then?

Love.

His brain screamed that word again and he stepped back. He was getting out of here. To hell with seeing the kid start school. To hell with standing by Rachel on this day. She might need a bit of support, and he couldn't even be sure of that, but he wasn't hanging around while his heart told him he'd fallen in love with the woman of his dreams. Not now, not ever. Been there, taken the hard knocks. And he didn't want to do that again.

'Ben?' Rachel had turned, was staring at him like he was something from Mars. 'Have you come to see Riley?'

Not me? her eyes seemed to ask with such deep sadness that his stomach clenched so tight it would take for ever before he'd be able to eat again.

Run, the cowardly half of his brain screamed. *Take control of yourself,* the other half muttered.

'Yeah,' he drawled, because that's all he could manage right now. 'Yeah.'

'That's cool.'

Cool? Him? With sweat prickling down his back? She was so wrong.

Rachel added, 'He'll be thrilled.' She shook the hand holding onto Riley like he was about to step off the edge of a cliff.

Then Riley turned, looked up, and shrieked at the top of his lungs, 'Ben, you came. I knew you would.' He tugged free of his mum's vice-like grip and leapt at Ben.

Ben rocked back as the small body slammed into him and stick-like arms strangled his waist. 'Hey, kid. I wasn't going to miss your first day at school.' He'd tried to.

Ben swung the boy up in his arms and peered into those enormous eyes nothing like the doc's staring back at him out of a pale face. So the kid was worried. Ben gave him a gentle shake and put him back on the concrete. 'You're going to have so much fun today.' He lifted his hand to high five Riley. 'Trust me?'

Riley's little hand tapped against his palm hard enough, but his voice wavered as he answered, 'I think so.'

'Look, your mates are waiting for you. With best friends like those scallywags a bloke can't go wrong. They won't let anything happen to you.' Ben flicked a finger under Riley's chin. 'You're going to have a blast.'

Rachel hovered over her boy, transferring to him some of her reluctance at letting go. Ben stood up, draped an arm around her shoulders and tucked her close to his side.

She was shaking and her voice wobbled. 'How dumb is this? This is a monumental day in my child's life and I can't let him go.'

Looking down, he saw where her teeth had made indentations in her bottom lip. Saw her eyes swimming with tears. His heart rolled. Love grabbed him and he tightened his grip on her. 'Bet your mother felt the same on your first day.'

'So she told me in an email this weekend. I thought she'd exaggerated, as she's prone to do.' Strength was returning to Rachel's voice, and the shakes were slowing. 'Thanks for coming. I really appreciate it.'

Of course, her husband should be here by her side, supporting her; egging his boy on and boosting his confidence. Did she still miss the guy hugely? As she had in the days after he'd died? Or was she moving on, putting that part of her life into a mental box to be taken out on days like today? He muttered, 'You're welcome.' Then he did something really stupid. 'Want to go for a coffee once Riley's settled?' His belly would be swimming in the stuff but in times of stress he'd do his bit.

'Mummy, I want to go inside now.' Riley cut through their conversation.

Rachel's shoulders lifted under his arm and she dredged up a rocky smile. 'Sure. If you're ready, so am I.'

'Are you coming?' Riley looked up at him, his little face trusting that he wouldn't be let down.

'Sure am.' Ben looked at Rachel, hoping he wouldn't see annoyance in her demeanour, and was relieved to see gratitude flashing back at him.

As the three of them walked up to the classroom door Ben had the weirdest feeling of being part of a family. Mum, Dad and the kid. He gasped, tripped over his own big feet. Family. Never in a million years would he have believed this possible.

Rachel glanced across at him, one eyebrow arched in question. 'You okay?'

Ben nodded. So much for staying away from

them, especially from Rachel. Here he was walking up the drive into a classroom, making sure they both coped with this bewildering event, wanting to be there to support Riley if he cried, needing to hold Rachel if *she* cried. And she was the one most likely to, he realised as he watched the emotions scudding across her face.

'Come in. Riley, you'll sit in the front row with Harry today. Best to be with someone you know, isn't it?' The teacher walked over to them as the trio hesitated on the doorstep, the eager chatter of twenty-odd children a sudden barrier to entry for Riley. And Rachel, Ben suspected.

Riley's chin dipped, touched his chest, but he managed to nod. His fist tightened in Ben's hand.

Ben dropped to his haunches. 'You okay, buddy?'

When Riley just stared at the floor, Ben looked around for Harry and waved him over. 'Why don't you two go sit down? Mum and I will be by the door until you feel happy about this.' Ben placed a hand on Riley's shoulder and turned him in the direction he needed to go.

Harry caught Riley's arm and dragged him away. 'Come on, Riley. If we hurry, Mrs Tualavi will read us a story.'

Ben led Rachel to some chairs and sat her down before taking the second chair and pulling it as close as possible to her. When he sat his thigh touched hers, his shoulder rubbed hers, and he covered her shaking hand lying on her thigh with his. 'He'll be fine in a few minutes. You watch.'

Rachel turned her gaze onto him. 'Thank you,' she mouthed. 'I really don't know what's come over me. Give me a submassive PE in one of my pregnant patients any day.'

Ben chuckled. 'A pulmonary embolism versus first day at school? Lady, you've got problems.'

Her eyes glinted at him. 'You know what a PE is.'

That was the trouble with forgetting to keep his guard up with this woman. She didn't miss a thing. He tried for a shrug, gave up. 'Who doesn't?'

Now those eyes were questioning. 'I doubt it's

something a policeman comes across in his day-to-day duties.'

Ben stretched his legs out in front of him while his brain raced through a multitude of answers, none of which he wanted to say out loud. Finally, 'I was married to a nurse.'

'So you had riveting discussions on medical conditions over a glass of wine at the end of a busy day policing and nursing.' Rachel's lips quirked in an annoying fashion, showing she wasn't angry with him.

'Something like that,' he muttered. Looking across to Riley, he hoped he could attract the boy's attention, pull a face at him, maybe make him laugh so as to distract his mother away from these unwelcome questions. But just when he needed the boy to be looking his way, Riley had finally become absorbed in his teacher and the story she was reading. Damn.

'Do you know someone who had PE? Did you lose someone because of it?' Rachel asked quietly. Suddenly her eyes widened and shock slammed into her.

'No, Rachel. Not Catrina.'

Rachel studied him long and hard before looking away and starting to fidget with the hem of her short skirt, folding it into pleats then smoothing it out again. 'Five minutes and then we can safely leave,' she whispered. 'And I'd love that coffee you mentioned.'

Double damn. Now he was for it. He could see the questions in her eyes. Ben deliberately checked his watch, looked amazed. 'Is that the time?' He *was* late for work but the boss knew where he was and would text him if he was needed.

A steely glint flashed back at him. 'Don't even think about getting out of your invitation.'

He tried a smile, one of those wide, open ones that usually seemed to turn her to putty in his hands. 'What about a rain check?' Some time next year would be good. Because she'd probably be gone by then.

Rachel lowered her head and looked up at him from under her lashes, in a kind of mock-growling way. 'I don't think so. I'm desperate for a decent coffee. This morning was bedlam in our house because of a certain young man so the best I could do was lukewarm instant coffee.' She shuddered delicately. 'You wouldn't want me starting my day without a proper caffeine fix, would you?'

Ben knew when he was beaten. And at least she'd cheered up immensely. 'You win.'

'Shall we sneak out?'

The kid didn't notice them going. Rachel, on the other hand, had that teary look again. 'He didn't even look up when I left.'

Baffled, Ben could only shake his head. 'Isn't that what you were hoping to achieve?'

'Yes, of course. But it doesn't do my ego a lot of good to be forgotten that quickly.' Her cheeks flushed red. 'Guess you think I'm nuts.'

'Completely.' Ben stopped beside her—uh, his—car. 'Meet you at Swampies for that caffeine. Follow me if you don't know where it is.'

He braced himself for the grilling he knew he was in for about his past.

* * *

Rachel stirred two packets of sugar crystals into her double-shot latte. 'I'm hanging out for this.'

Ben stretched his legs to the side of the table, looking very relaxed. Except it was an act. His fingers holding his teaspoon were white, and he'd been stirring his coffee for minutes now.

She tapped the back of his hand with her forefinger. 'It's okay. I'm not going to quiz you about your medical knowledge.'

His spoon stopped doing circuits of the cup. 'You're not?'

Leaning back in her chair, she studied the man she'd come to care far too much about. She'd missed him terribly this past week and she wasn't about to wreck whatever time she got with him by asking something that would obviously upset him. If he wanted to talk, he would. If not, she could wait until he was ready, if that ever happened. Right now she owed him for turning up at the school.

'Thank you for this morning. I was struggling with the whole scenario and you made me feel a lot better.'

'I trained as a doctor. A GP.'

At first Rachel wasn't sure she'd heard right. She hadn't been expecting Ben to tell her anything about himself right now. Then his pronouncement really sank in. And she wasn't surprised. 'I figured you had some medical training.'

Ben was watching her, caution all over his face. 'Hard to hide at times.'

Why would he want to? 'I guess. Medicine becomes a part of us, doesn't it?' What had gone wrong? Rachel sipped her coffee. She couldn't, wouldn't, ask.

'It's not a career for just anybody. Certainly not me.' He drained his cup, stood up. 'Coming?'

Rachel tried to quickly gulp down her coffee but it was too hot. The cup banged onto the saucer and she pushed it aside. Not her morning for caffeine fixes. 'You're really late for work?'

'They know where I am. Let's walk.' He took her hand and headed out of the café, turning towards the beach.

Rachel left her shoes on the edge of the sand

and they meandered along the water's edge, occasionally letting the wavelets rush across their toes.

Just as she was about to say she should be heading to the hospital, Ben suddenly cut her short.

'I wanted to be a doctor ever since an accident involving a shepherd on Dad's farm. At first Dad was very disappointed because my brother had already indicated he wasn't going to stay on the farm either. We were both exceptional at science. Got that from our mother.'

'So what happened to the farm?' Wrong question, when Ben was finally talking about himself.

'My sister is the farmer of the family. Absolutely loves the hard work and being outdoors all the time. The lifestyle suits her kids too. She got married well after having the children, reckoned she was too busy for a wedding and the honeymoon her man wanted.'

'So your father didn't have to sell the farm, then?' She was intrigued to learn anything about Ben and his family.

Ben grunted something that sounded like a

laugh. 'Not to outsiders, anyway. My brother-in-law's a wealthy stockbroker who adores her. He works from home and is chief cook and bottle-washer, looks after the kids, and generally frees her up to farm.'

'Sounds perfect.' A twist of envy curled through her. Some people had all the luck. And Ben? 'So you went to med school.'

'Yeah.' His sigh would've been heard a kilometre away if not for the plane coming in to land at the nearby airport. 'I did. At first it was fine. I learned fast and easily. Loved the hustle and long, grinding hours of training and studying.' He stared along the beach in the direction they were walking. 'Even enjoyed being able to make people better. But those I couldn't save got to me every time.'

'I think we all feel like that. If we don't believe we could save everyone who comes to us for help then we'd falter, begin questioning what we do.'

Ben's strides lengthened and she stretched out beside him, trying to keep up, knowing there was more to come.

Finally he continued. 'The surprise for me was that I wanted the continuity that comes with treating people and their families, watching the kids grow up, the parents getting older. I found the treat 'em and discharge 'em of ED left me unfulfilled, and I hated the level of distress many patients suffered in there. So I became a GP.' His voice faded.

When Rachel looked across at him the eyes that met hers were bleak.

'But...' He sighed and stopped to stare over the water. 'This is so crazy. I've never been able to endure watching other people suffer. When the shepherd was injured way back I was gutted that I couldn't spare him the pain from the quad bike crushing him. All I could do was race home, running as fast as I could for more than seven kilometres to get help.

'Everyone said I did the right thing and that if I hadn't done that the guy would've died. I revelled in the praise but hated that I'd not been able to deal with what I saw in the man's eyes.'

She wanted to stop him talking if it would take

that look away, but it wouldn't. He'd started on this now and if she knew Ben at all she knew he would see his tale out to the bitter end.

He turned to look down at her. 'I believed that if I became a doctor and learned to make people better, I'd get over this thing. I never did.'

Which was why he played the role of hero all the time. She was no psychologist but anyone would see that. 'So when did you resign and take up policing?'

'After Catrina died. If it had been hard to watch people suffering before then, afterwards it was impossible. At the scene of the accident I had to watch her eyes fill with the pain of her ribs ripping her lungs to shreds every time she breathed. The agony was insurmountable. She pleaded with me to help her, to stop the pain, and there was nothing I could do other than hold her hand. I was trapped in the cavity between my seat and the engine.'

Rachel's hand gripped Ben's as she tried to give him solace. Too little, way too late, but what else could she do?

Ben shuddered. 'That's what I remember the most. That, and the guilt for wanting to look away. I had to force myself to maintain eye contact with her until finally, thankfully, her eyelids fell shut. What she suffered was unbearable. For both of us.'

Rachel slipped her arms around him, held him close to her, feeling the tension rippling through his belly, his chest, along his arms. All she could give him was her warmth, her softness. It wasn't anywhere near enough.

She had no idea how long they stood together like that. Finally Ben stepped back, sniffed. 'Look at me. A scratch under two metres tall with shoulders three pick handles wide, and I cannot endure seeing other people's pain.'

'That's nothing to be ashamed of.' She leaned back in his arms and looked into his dark eyes. 'I refuse to believe otherwise.'

On his belt his cellphone beeped. He tugged it off, read the text message. 'I'm needed at the station.'

They began retracing their steps.

Rachel thought about what he'd told her, about the kind, caring man he was. She had no doubts at all that Ben would have been a fantastic doctor. He had the intelligence, the mannerisms that made patients feel comfortable, the kind of enquiring mind that wouldn't accept first results in cases that required more digging, and he certainly wouldn't refuse to listen to his colleagues. But he'd probably carried those characteristics into his new career.

Now that she knew his story Rachel could understand why he was in the police force in a small country where apparently not a lot went wrong, where he wasn't required to make life-threatening decisions on other people's behalves on a regular basis. And yet he still leapt in where needed to save someone in danger. That was something she couldn't ignore. Not when she and her son lived with the consequences of Jamie acting in the same manner.

'What time's your clinic?' Ben murmured.

They were back at the car park, standing by the car. Rachel nodded. 'In ten minutes.'

'How is Liu? Have you heard?' Ben's brow creased.

'I spoke to her oncologist in Auckland yesterday, who told me she's halfway through her chemo and hassling all the staff about when she can come home.'

'She'll be missing her girls. I'm surprised they didn't all move to Auckland with her for the duration.'

Rachel sighed. 'I guess that's one of the hardships of living here.'

'But you're making a difference. If you hadn't started those clinics then Liu's outlook would've been very grim.' Ben tapped her shoulder. 'I've really got to go.'

'Thanks for telling me about your past.' She watched him slide into his truck, tug the seat belt over his shoulder, start the engine. His wave was short and distracted as he drove out onto the road.

She understood Ben far more now. But where did that leave her? Still facing the fact he could do something thoughtlessly dangerous and not come home at the end of the day. Whenever a situation arose, like hauling those men off the reef, he'd jump in boots and all. A hero. Another damned hero.

Her heart ached. With love. With despair. She still had to pull away from Ben. Now. While she still could. It was probably even more imperative because he wasn't ever going to change. Permanently finishing what they had going on between them would hurt. Hugely. But at least she wouldn't be going to his funeral after one of his heroic tricks.

CHAPTER TWELVE

MISSION accomplished without even trying. Ben had given Rachel the perfect reason to stay away from him.

So what was the problem? He should be pleased Rachel was about to wake up to his shortcomings and take matters in hand. At least it would be easier at the end of the day if he didn't have to sneak into his house after dark, trying to avoid her. For the past few days he'd deliberately hung around the police station or gone for a feed with his colleagues to fill in time until it was safe to go home and not have to deal with his neighbour.

That hadn't stopped him aching to go over and hold Rachel, to trace those sweet lips with his finger before kissing them both into another world. Today he'd done something really, really stupid. He'd gone along to be with Rachel for the kid's first day at school. Hell, he'd stood there, holding Riley's hand, watching the tears and confusion in Rachel's eyes and wishing he could hug all that sorrow away. They'd been so together, the three of them.

Like a family. The very thing he'd been trying to avoid for years. And he'd walked right into it, not stopping to really, seriously think about the consequences, not even once considering how he'd feel afterwards. He'd missed them both so much in the days leading up to this monumental blunder, and then he'd capped everything off with a full-blown confession about what a useless shell of a man he was.

'Hey, Ben, are you here or what?'

Ben blinked, looked up from his desk into the observant gaze of his sidekick, Harley. 'Do I look like an apparition?'

'So are we going?'

'Going where?' Ben shook the images of Rachel out of his head and concentrated on what the sergeant had to say.

'To arrest Hawthorne.'

'Now? Am I missing something here?'

Harley shook his head. 'And you asked if you were an apparition. We've just had a ten-minute, one-sided conversation about Operation Stoat.' Harley slapped his paw on top of the huge file sitting on Ben's desk. 'We've got all the info we need. We've got the warrant to search his house and factory as of half an hour ago. The boys are kitted up and raring to go. So, are we on?'

Ben stood up, snatched up the keys to the police truck. 'Absolutely. Anything you've told me in the last few minutes that I need to know?' There shouldn't be. He had been working long hours on this unusual case.

Harley snorted. 'Man, you sure know how to make a bloke feel good.'

Action time. Taking in their man for questioning, and then the challenge of outwitting him— bring it on. Just what the doctor ordered. Humph. Definitely not the doctor who'd been rattling his brain so persistently over the past few months.

'Saw you standing with Rachel and the lad at

school this morning.' Harley headed outside, not waiting for Ben's acerbic reply.

Driving through town, Ben put his personal life on hold and concentrated on the job. If he didn't, mistakes could be made and he was done with mistakes. He needed to get his head together and decide what the hell he was going to do about his future. But not at this moment when his colleagues relied on him to back them up. Keep them safe. Because one thing they'd known about Hawthorne right from the start of this investigation was that he had firearms stashed in his house.

After weeks of surveillance, and working with the fraud squad in Auckland, they were finally nabbing Hawthorne for scamming the old and the innocent out of their money.

Beside him Harley waved to an old man shuffling along the footpath. 'Poor old boy. We might be arresting Hawthorne but it's cold comfort to Toko. What he wants is his money back so he can continue to pay for his grandkids' education in New Zealand.'

That's what made Ben angry. Furious, even. Hawthorne didn't give a fig for the heartache he caused when he stole the hard-earned savings from the locals. The slimeball was a smooth-talker who conned people into investing in his non-existent companies by offering higher returns than banks did. And while people shouldn't be so naïve, it didn't make what Hawthorne had done right. He'd fleeced the islanders living in the Cooks and in Auckland. Hawthorne was one of them. His mother lived in Muri in a shack because her son had divested her of every cent she'd had.

'Time's up, buddy. It's our turn to take something from you. Your freedom.' Ben raced up the sweeping drive of one the most opulent houses on the island and leapt out of the truck. Time for action. Time to save the locals from the Stoat. Time to do something he could be proud of.

Riley fell asleep in his dinner.

Rachel ran a hand over his head, smiling at the soft, springy feel of his too-long hair. Pride at her little warrior's ability to cope with everything life handed him welled up, brought tears to her eyes.

Knock, knock. Ben stood at the back door, his face unreadable. 'Hi,' he whispered. 'I promised Riley I'd see him tonight. Looks like his big day got the better of him.'

'He's exhausted. But he loved school and hasn't stopped talking since he came home. Apparently I know nothing about anything. Mrs Tualava is the current expert on any subject you care to raise.' Her smile widened.

'Teacher's privilege.' Ben grinned and stepped inside. 'Want me to carry him down to his bedroom?'

'I'd love you to. He's getting far too heavy for me to haul around.' Rachel led the way so she could turn down the sheet.

Ben placed Riley carefully on the bed. 'You going to undress him?'

She nodded and reached to slip Riley's shirt over his head while Ben held him upright. Her hands slid across Ben's as she lifted the bottom of the shirt, and she paused, aware of the sparks zipping between them. She'd missed Ben's touch. Missed his kisses. Missed making love with him. It would only take one little movement and she'd throw herself into his arms. And she'd vowed not to do that. Ever again. And after today? She'd be an idiot if she did. Her heart hammered in her throat.

Ben waited quietly, not moving at all, as though holding his breath. Did he know the turmoil roiling through her? Could he see it in her eyes?

Rachel averted her gaze and tugged Riley's shirt off. Leaning over, she placed a kiss on his soft cheek. 'Goodnight, sweetheart.' Reluctantly she turned for the door where she paused to look back, and gasped. Not fair. So not fair.

Ben had dropped to his haunches beside the bed. His hand rested on Riley's sheet-covered shoulder. 'Goodnight, kid. Glad the day worked out for you. You're growing up fast.'

'Too fast.' Rachel didn't know she'd spoken aloud until Ben turned to look at her, lifting one eyebrow in query.

'You want to hold him back?' he whispered.

'Don't be silly.' She headed for the kitchen and the salad she'd begun preparing while Riley had eaten his hastily put-together dinner.

'Silly, eh?' Ben stood behind her.

Close behind her. She could feel his breaths on her bare neck. Smell that man scent of his. Desire slammed into her. A lifetime without him yawned before her. Her insides were quivering so much she should've liquefied. Her body hankered after his touch. And now he was within inches of her, the heat radiating out from him, sucking her nearer, promising untold pleasures. Totally undoing all her resolve to end this now, tonight. Ben was her ultimate dream guy—passionate, sexy, caring, a community man. Her ultimate fear: a blasted hero.

She spun away. Struggled for control over the desire that wouldn't abate. Logic might tell her to keep away, but there was nothing logical about how her body responded to the sight and sound of him. She wanted him. All of him. Now. In her bed, inside her.

Leaning back against the bench, she folded her

arms under her breasts and tried to ignore where his gaze cruised. 'Thank you for coming over to see Riley. He'll be sorry he missed you. He went to find you earlier but you hadn't come home.' And she'd had to listen to a barrage of Ben this and Ben that, interspersed with Mrs Tualava this, Mrs Tualava that.

'Had an eventful day at work.' A frown marred his beautiful face as he studied her.

'So I heard.' The anger she'd held down all day sprang loose. There'd been a shoot-out involving police at some businessman's house earlier in the day and she'd spent hours barely able to breathe, hardly functioning at all, as she'd waited to hear if Ben was all right. When the ambulance had arrived at the hospital with one slightly wounded policeman on board, she'd raced out to see who it was. The relief she'd felt when she saw it wasn't Ben had been quickly replaced by anger.

'I guess you did.' Ben stared at her. 'I'm sorry. You'd have liked me to call you.'

Her anger returned in an instant. 'Too damned

right I would've. Did you honestly think I wouldn't care? Wouldn't be worried about you?'

'We finally made an arrest in a fraud case we've been working on for a long time. A local who's been ripping a lot of money off family and friends.'

'Oh, right. Ben to the rescue.' All the excuse he needed for ignoring basic manners. And she'd thought they might be able to get along as friends after this morning.

He crossed to the fridge. 'Got any beer in here?'

Why didn't he just go home? Leave her to get on with her life? 'I'll have one too.' She took the proffered bottle that he'd twisted the cap off, carefully avoiding any contact with those fingers. The chilled liquid was like nectar in her dry mouth, on her parched throat. It didn't go so well with her churning stomach.

'Rachel, it was a very controlled situation at the house.'

'The man shot at one of your colleagues.'

'Wrong. He didn't even pick up a weapon. We knew there were guns in that house and proceeded accordingly. He had to be taken into custody. That's all there was to it.'

Bang. Her beer bottle cracked hard on the bench top. Ben did not belong with her. Not now, not ever. 'And the cop who was injured?'

'Got knocked down by another man running away from the scene. Cracked his head against a balustrade.' Ben grimaced. 'I guess the rumour mill has been working overtime on this.'

'Which is why it would've been nice to have heard from you.'

'I can't do this.' Ben stood in front of her, looking wistful as he scrutinised her face. Looking for what? Forgiveness? 'I'd better go.'

'I'm sorry, Ben, but I won't live with knowing you're always ready to leap in saving people all the time.'

He reached across the chasm between them, his finger lifting her chin. 'I know, Rachel. I know.'

And then he was gone, leaving her chilled in the warm kitchen, her heart hurting so badly she was afraid it would explode.

* * *

'How's that arm?' Rachel asked Lissie as they sat on the stern of the boat, watching the kids swimming and diving.

'Now the pain's gone, it's more of a nuisance than anything. I still can't believe I slipped on that banana skin. That only happens in kids' joke books.' Lissie glared at the cast encasing her right arm. 'And I'm itching fit to bust underneath this.'

Rachel forced a chuckle. 'I admit I didn't believe Harry when he told me.'

'Mum, look at me.' A dripping Riley leapt head first into the water from the divers' platform on the back of the boat.

Rachel shook her head. 'He's fearless. Anyone would think he'd been swimming all his life, not three months.'

'Better than being hesitant.' Lissie lay back on a cushion. 'Right now I'd give anything to be able to leap in with them. It's so hot out here.'

The boat belonged to one of the charter companies Pita's family owned. Today had been unusually quiet so after school Pita had offered to bring everyone out to the far side of the lagoon where the water was deeper and more exciting for swimming. The kids were having an awesome time dive bombing each other, something they couldn't do inshore.

Pita was tinkering with some dive gear, keeping it in pristine condition. 'You'd think those kids would lose their voices after a while.'

'If only.' Rachel smiled. 'Riley seems to be running on long-life batteries. He never stops talking. I can't believe he's the same quiet boy I brought out from London.'

Pita glanced up. 'He's come a long way, that's for sure. I heard Ben talking to him about fishing the other day and you'd think he'd been offering the moon.'

'When was that?' Riley hadn't mentioned anything to her. She'd barely seen Ben since he'd stormed out of her house nearly three weeks ago. Three difficult weeks when she'd struggled to hold onto her determination not to beg him to come back.

'On the beach outside my dive shop after school a couple of days back. Ben had all our kids with him. Riley seems to hang onto every word he utters.' Pita wiped a smear of grease off a dive tank. 'A kid can't go wrong with a man like Ben influencing him.'

A knot formed in Rachel's tummy. 'True, as long as Riley doesn't get too attached to him.'

'You thinking of moving on some time soon?' Lissie asked. 'I thought you were settled.'

'I am. I love this place, but who knows what's in the future?' Not a permanent relationship with Ben, for one thing. 'I never intended coming here for ever. Don't get me wrong, but I do think the day will come when I'll want to go back to working in a big hospital.' Her gaze cruised the calm water, seeking out her boy amongst his friends, finding him.

Face down, arms and legs spread wide. Fear clutched her throat, balled in her belly, popped bumps on her skin. 'Riley,' she screamed as she scrambled to her feet. 'Riley! I'm coming,' she called, even though she knew he couldn't hear her. She jumped. Off the stern of the boat. Into deeper water than she'd ever been in before. And plummeted straight to the bottom. Down, down, down. Panic gripped her. Too deep. She should be on the top. Water surrounded her, terrified her. Her feet kicked, her hands scrabbled around. *Don't breathe. For God's sake, don't breathe. You'll drown.*

Kicking hard, she aimed for the surface. Where was the surface? Down here everything looked the same. Something brushed her calf and she opened her mouth to scream. Salt water rushed in. She wanted to gasp, spit it out, but in a rational moment knew she couldn't.

Then suddenly she popped up into bright sunlight. Blinking, gasping, she flailed around, reaching blindly for the boat, anything solid to hang onto. 'Help!' she shrieked when her desperate fingers found nothing more solid than water.

Strong hands caught around her waist, held her. 'I've got you.'

The most welcome voice in the world. 'Ben?' she choked, then coughed salt water from her mouth.

'Riley?' she squeaked.

'Safe as houses.'

'But his face was in the water. Where is he?' Chill fear shook her.

'I promise you, he's fine. He's playing with the other kids still. He didn't see you jump in.' Ben pushed her towards the boat. 'Take Pita's hand so he can pull you on board.'

A hand appeared before her streaming eyes. 'Here, hang onto me.' Pita's voice was as much a lifeline as his hand. 'You're okay now. Guess you've never stepped off a boat into deep water before.'

'Never. And I won't do it again either.'

Ben's hands fell away from her waist and panic rose in her throat. Then he was pushing her back-side upwards at the same time Pita pulled from above. In seconds she was sprawled unceremoniously across the deck, coughing and shaking. Pushing up on her elbows, she scanned the sea for Riley, heard him before she saw him. He was laughing and splashing and diving. 'Riley, come here. Now,' she yelled.

Lissie knelt beside her. 'Rachel, are you okay?

You scared the daylights out of me. You dropped
like a rock.'

'I need Riley.'

Ben swam across to the kids, plucked Riley
from the group and made a game of bringing him
across to the boat. 'Your mum wants to talk to
you.' Ben's eyes were filled with understanding
and concern as he lifted Riley up to her. There
was something else in his gaze too that she refused to acknowledge.

'Thanks,' she whispered as she wrapped her
shaking arms around her boy. She wouldn't think
about what was lurking in Ben's eyes. She'd hold
Riley, talk to him, make sure he really was alive
and well. 'Riley, love.' And then she didn't know
what to say. Minutes ago she'd thought Riley was
drowning. Now he squirmed and wriggled in her
too-tight hold, wanting to be free to get back to
his friends.

She'd made a fool of herself. Worse, she'd jumped
into the water without thought for her own safety.
She could've drowned. Then where would Riley
have been? Parentless. She was no better than

Jamie. Or Ben. No, that wasn't fair. Ben would've checked the depth before jumping in, would've made sure there weren't any rocks lurking below the surface. Ben was a lot more cautious than she'd just proved herself to be.

'Mummy, can I go now?' When she nodded dumbly he leapt free and raced to the platform. 'Watch me.'

She opened her mouth to call him back, to say, No, don't jump. Nothing came out. All words had dried up. Riley was safe, and not because of her.

'Did you see me being a starfish?' Riley spread his arms and legs. 'Like this.'

'Yes, love, I saw you.' *And acted impulsively because I thought you were drowning.*

'I'll show you again.' Eagerness filled his eyes.

No. Absolutely not. Stay with me. Her heart couldn't withstand another shock like that last one. But she wasn't being fair. Riley had done nothing wrong. And to stop him would require an explanation that might undermine his confidence. 'I guess.'

'Watch.' Riley leapt high, legs and arms spread

wide. Water sprayed over her as his body cannoned into the sea.

Lissie rubbed Rachel's shoulder. 'They think they're invincible.'

'I guess that's better than feeling afraid all the time. But hard on their parents.' She turned to look at Lissie. 'Are you ever terrified that something terrible might happen to one of yours?'

'All the time.' Lissie wrapped a dry towel around Rachel. 'You're shivering enough to shake the boat.'

Tears threatened at the simple kindness from her friend. 'Thanks,' she croaked. Seemed she was thanking everyone at the moment. Something else occurred to her. 'Where did Ben come from?'

'He was approaching in his runabout from the front, away from the kids, when you did your elephant dive.'

'That's what I felt like as I hit the bottom.'

A light knock on the side of the boat and the end of a rope flicked through the air, caught neatly by Pita, to be tied onto the railing. Then

Ben stepped over from his runabout. 'I was a few metres away, bringing Pita the engine oil he'd been waiting all week for, when you leapt overboard.' He sat down beside her. 'You okay?'

Rachel straightened her spine, fighting the inclination to sink against Ben's strong, protective body. She didn't deserve his comfort, his concern. 'I'm really shaken. Riley was lying face down in the water.' She swallowed salty saliva. 'Being a starfish, apparently.'

'And you reacted like any parent would.'

Like a goddamned hero. Heroine. She shivered. 'I guess. I didn't even think about anything except saving Riley.'

'I know.'

She waited for his remonstration. She deserved it. One, for acting so spontaneously. Two, for all the things she'd said to Ben about not being careful. 'I'm so stupid.'

'No, you're a mother,' he said, then draped an arm over her shoulders and tugged her close to him. Her resistance evaporated quicker than a bubble bursting and she pressed into his warm, muscular body.

'Sorry, for everything.'

'Shh. It doesn't matter.'

They sat there, saying nothing more, watching the kids until Lissie called them all aboard. It was time to head home.

'How about I take you and Riley with me?' Ben suggested to Rachel. 'I've got some chops to put on the barbeque at home.'

Was this a new beginning? *No, you can't start over. You'd have to go through all the pain to get to this point again.* This was a continuation of what had started the night Ben had brought Effie to her.

Rachel said nothing on the way in to shore, or as Ben drove them home, towing the runabout. She was quiet while she showered and put on navy shorts and a white sleeveless shirt. Exhaustion had caught up with Riley and he could barely pull his pyjamas on. Rachel didn't insist he eat a proper dinner. Her heart wasn't in it. He'd make up for it tomorrow at breakfast.

Ben arrived with the chops as she came out of Riley's bedroom where he lay sound asleep, sprawled in his latest favourite position—like a starfish.

She took the beer Ben offered and tossed together a salad while he warmed up the barbeque. All the while a picture of Riley with his face in the water ran over and over in her mind. And on the periphery of that picture she saw Jason next to Riley, another starfish in the making. Why hadn't she looked harder, checked out the other kids, before leaping in? She'd have understood what they were doing, would've at least hesitated and maybe asked Lissie or Pita if they were okay.

So this was how Jamie had acted that day. Why he'd died. He'd acted instinctively when he'd seen his colleague in danger. As Ben had done with those kids who'd nearly drowned— would've drowned if he hadn't dived in to rescue them. It didn't make the thoughtlessness of the act right, but it was now totally understandable. She'd done the same thing, reacting the moment it had crashed into her brain that Riley was in trouble.

Rachel made her way outside and sat down on the top step. She sucked in a shaky breath, filling her lungs to capacity, pushing her chest up and lifting her chin. 'Ben, I made a huge mistake out there today.'

He took up the space beside her, sitting close, stretching his legs down the stairs. 'It's okay.' His voice caressed her, his breathing warmed her cold forehead when he leaned close. 'Really okay. You're safe. Riley's safe. No harm done.'

'But I shouldn't have said those things to you, about you.'

'Shh. I understand.'

He did. She got that at least. He wasn't mad at her for being a hypocrite. He understood. 'Thank you.'

They sat some more. Sipped their beers. Watched the sky light up red and orange as the sun let go of the day. Finally she murmured, 'You were there for me.' She clicked her fingers. 'Just like that. You came out of nowhere and grabbed me. I've never felt so relieved, so safe.'

'You gave me a hell of a shock when you went straight down like that.'

'You always seem to turn up when I need you.' She picked at the label on her bottle. 'Like Riley's first day at school, when I was breaking into tiny pieces inside and there you were, standing tall and strong beside me.'

Like a partner. Not just a lover. Someone vested in her life, and her son's life. A man she could envisage sharing her future with. If only she could let go of the past.

Beside her Ben sighed and stretched his legs further. 'I need to ask you something.'

Something in his tone made her study him closely. 'Yes?'

'Are you going to stay on when your contract's up?'

'Definitely. Riley's the happiest he's been in two years. I don't want to upset that.' She hauled air into her lungs. 'And I'm not ready to go anywhere else yet. Maybe not for a long time.' This was the perfect life for her, with one exception. Ben wasn't a part of it.

'I've been offered a promotion. One that might eventually take me back home for a while. But not for the next year or two.'

'That's great news. Isn't it?'

'I haven't accepted yet, but I want to.'

The stars started making an appearance. They sat in silence again. Then Rachel felt as though her heart was blocking her throat. She loved this man. It was as simple, as complex as that. She turned to Ben, caught his hand between hers. 'We're great together but I'm afraid. Of us. For us.'

His gaze met hers, open and honest. 'So am I, Rachel.'

'You are?' She was staring at him, stunned he'd admit to the same thing.

Ben drew his legs up, dropped his free hand over his knees. 'Yes. Very afraid.'

'I love you, Ben,' she whispered. 'But I never want to go through that pain again. Losing Jamie was the worst thing that has ever happened to me.'

His big hand engulfed her slim one. 'I wouldn't survive something like what happened to Catrina a second time either.' His thumb began tracing circles on the back of her hand. Soft, caring, loving strokes that stilled her whacking heart, gave her a sense of peace despite the issues lying between them.

Then he lifted his head, those black eyes locking with hers. 'But I love you too, and I can't walk away from you. That would hurt as much. I want to live with you, have a future with you. I'm ready to take a chance on happiness. Are you?' He hesitated, caution creeping into his honest gaze. 'I'll wait for you, for as long as it takes.'

Her lips formed a smile, a smile that came from deep inside somewhere around her heart. The heaviness that had been pressing down on her since she'd made that mistake with Riley on the water left her, and she sat up straighter. 'I'm right beside you, with you, on the same page. It's already too late to walk away, if I ever had a chance to. From that night when you banged down my door and brought Effie inside I've known deep down you were meant to be a part of my life.'

'I knocked. I didn't bang down your door.' He grinned tentatively. 'Does this mean what I think it does? That we're connected? We're going forward together?'

'Try staying away from me and see what happens.' The happiness bubble that had been slow to grow suddenly ballooned so large she couldn't swallow. 'I'm only half-afraid of the future now that we're together.'

Then Ben was kissing her like he'd never stop. Demanding kisses that asked for reassurance, and gave back reassurance of his love. Kisses that spoke of the past, of their future. Kisses that melted her bones, liquefied her muscles, and tipped her into him. This man she loved so much. This man she was prepared to take another chance at life with. 'I love you,' she murmured against his mouth.

CHAPTER THIRTEEN

Six months later

'YOU may kiss your bride,' the marriage celebrant told Ben.

'At last. The bit I've been waiting for all day.' Ben grinned at Mrs Armstrong.

'You've been kissing me most of the day.' Rachel grinned back.

'Ah, but I haven't kissed my wife.' Ben leaned in, his lips skidding across hers in a slow, tantalising way. Then he pulled back.

'That's it? I got married for that?' She couldn't stop grinning at him, like one of those clowns at the show where people stuffed balls in their mouths to win prizes.

'You think?' Ben hauled her up close, his body touching the length of hers. His mouth claimed her lips, his tongue danced with hers, his hands spread across her back, searing her skin through the silk of her wedding dress. Rachel forgot to breathe, forgot where she was, as his kiss deepened and started fires of desire under her skin.

'Okay, you two, we get the picture,' Pita called from somewhere behind them.

'Yeah, Mummy, that's gross.'

Rachel leaned back in Ben's arms and glanced down at her son. 'You wait until it's your turn, young man.'

'*Eww.* I'm never going to kiss a girl.'

Lissie approached, tears oozing from the corners of her eyes, and pulled Rachel away from her husband to wrap her in a big hug. 'I'm so happy for you. You two really are so meant to be together.'

Rachel hugged her friend back as hard as she could. 'Thanks for making me come all the way out here. It's been the best move I could've made.'

'Time for photos, everyone.' The celebrant, who also stepped in as the photographer, started rounding them up and directing them down closer to the water's edge.

'Why did you make us wear these gorgeous shoes when the guys are barefoot?' Lissie asked.

'Because they are gorgeous shoes,' Rachel answered as she peered down her summer-sky-blue satin gown to her perfectly matched shoes. 'And because I don't get to dress up very often any more so I wanted to go all out. But the sand is a bit of a problem, isn't it?'

'As long as we get it out before we start dancing at the restaurant.'

Ben tapped Lissie on the shoulder. 'Do I get a hug too?'

'Absolutely.' Lissie leapt at Ben while Pita gave Rachel an equally enthusiastic hug.

Riley raced across the sand to his grandparents. 'Come on, Granddad, Grandma. You've got to be in the pictures.'

Rachel still couldn't believe her parents had flown all the way out here for her wedding. How her mother had persuaded Dad to come was beyond her. And over by the coconut palms Ben's brother shoved her brother's wheelchair through the sand towards them, while her sister-in-law chattered with Ben's sister.

Happiness bubbled along her veins. Never in a million years would she have dreamed she'd be this happy. Ben looked absolutely stunning in his white, open-necked silk shirt and tan trousers. The bare feet didn't detract at all.

An island wedding. How many had she seen happening all around Rarotonga? Every one of them beautiful, but none as beautiful as this one. From the white hibiscus in her hair to the three boys dressed in matching white shirts—white for how long?—and tan pants. And of course bare feet. How much further could she be from her previous life?

'Rachel, you're absolutely glowing.' Her mother kissed her cheek. 'I'm really happy for you. Ben's a wonderful man.'

'Thanks, Mum. He is kind of special, isn't he?' She turned to her father. 'Hey, Dad. How are you doing?'

'What's wrong with getting married in a church

or a hall? Even a restaurant?' He shook his head.
'I've got sand in my socks.'

Rachel laughed and kissed his forehead. 'I love
you, you old grouch.' Nothing, no one, would
spoil this day for her.

Her father blinked rapidly. 'You're my girl. You
know that, don't you?' And he kissed her on both
cheeks. 'Your mother bribed me into coming.'

'With what?' When her father's face coloured
she hastily added, 'No, don't tell me.' Rachel fin-
gered where his lips had touched her. Miracles
did happen. The last time her father had done that
had been before her brother's accident.

Ben took her elbow, drew her close. 'I saw that.
You okay?'

Her eyes were swimming when she looked up
into her husband's face. 'Couldn't be better.'

'Mummy.' Riley raced towards them. 'The lady
wants to take pictures and you've got to be in
them. You too, Daddy.'

Ben tripped over his own feet.

Rachel stilled in shock.

Around them the excited chatter slowed, quieted.

Riley skidded to a halt in front of Rachel and Ben. He placed one hand in Rachel's and one in Ben's. 'Come on,' he exhorted.

Ben dropped to his haunches and bundled Riley into a hug. 'I'm Daddy?'

'Of course you are. Isn't he, Mummy? If you're living in our house then you must be.'

Ben stood, still holding his son, and turned to Rachel. 'I couldn't have asked for anything more. A beautiful wife and a wonderful son.'

She leaned into him and whispered, 'What about another child? In seven months' time?'

Riley squealed as he was squashed between them when Ben all but devoured Rachel. Tears poured down Ben's cheeks. 'I love you so much. All I've got to offer you is my heart.'

Rachel smiled. That would do just fine.

* * * * *